No greater love

Pastor Derek Jones

The following is a work of fiction. It is intended to give the reader a clearer understanding of some of the features of the New Covenant that they might have overlooked.

The New Covenant is perhaps best understood in the context of a marriage. As you study this book I pray that you will pay extra attention to the various parts of the Hebrew wedding ceremony. In it you will find new meaning to the promises of God that are recorded in the sacred Scriptures.

The wedding ceremony consisted of several parts.

First there was the Shiddukhin. It is the choosing of the bride.

Second was the Mohar. This was the "Bride-price." This was what the value of the bride was to the father of the groom.

Third was the Mattan. This was a "Love-gift" which was given by the groom. This was so that she would not be beholden to her parents for anything.

Fourth was the Ketubbah. This was the "Marriage contract". It stipulated the rules for the engagement and the marriage itself.

Fifth was the Kiddushin. This was the time where the bride proved her fidelity, and the groom prepared his home for his bride.

The sixth part was the Nissuin. It was the wedding ceremony itself.

It is my fervent hope that the reader will understand certain things after reading this book:

First: is that God instituted marriage as a divine covenant. It was His idea.

Second: God's great promises to the church are all in accord with the Hebrew marriage covenant. His promises are still in effect, and will be until Jesus returns for His bride.

Third: only those who meet the conditions will be recognized as the bride of Christ

Once again let me emphasize that this is a work of fiction. None of the events mentioned happened.

However, the facts of the Word of God and the marriage ceremony are true.

This book is the first part of a two-volume set dealing with the Hebrew wedding ceremony. The second book is entitled "No Greater Love, The Bride of Christ" it goes into greater detail concerning the various parts of the ceremony. It is also available online and through Amazon, Barnes and Nobles and other fine retailers

No Greater Love
Tamar's Story

Pastor Derek Jones

No Greater Love

Tamar's Story

Chapter 1: Abiel and his son............................7

Chapter 2: Tamar...15

Chapter 3: Abiel tells Jedidiah.........................23

Chapter 4: The lovers meet.............................37

Chapter 5: Dannah..47

Chapter 6: Tamar is unfaithful........................63

Chapter 7: Abiel and Jedidiah in Jerusalem.....81

Chapter 8: My redeemer lives!......................101

Chapter 9: A tough choice to make...............123

Chapter 10: The wedding...............................145

Epilogue; A family is born...........................161

From the Pastor; God's plan..........................165

Chapter one: Abiel and his son

In the days when Judah was ruled by the kings there was a man of prominence who lived in Jerusalem. His name was Abiel, and he had one son whose name was Jedidiah.

Abiel dearly loved his son. As he grew to manhood Abiel desired more than anything for his son to be happily married.

Jedidiah was everything that Abiel hoped that he would be. He loved the Lord God, and loved his fellow man. There was no fault in him.

They lived in Jerusalem, and Abiel worked hard to keep his son from being corrupted by the evil influences of the city.

Jerusalem in those days had become the seat of rebellion against God. The temple worship continued just as it had since the days of King Solomon. But the priest and the people were merely going through the motions. The people had forgotten about loving God. Now they only served Him out of a sense of duty.

The love of God was no longer even in their thoughts. As a result of losing their love for God they had also lost their love for God's people. Murder and robberies had become common. Rape and even incest happened with regularity.

Many of the wealthier families were guilty of extortion. They held the poorest down by charging high fees and interest on everything they bought.

Even the priests were guilty of taking bribes from corrupt officials to get them to give false testimonies. Many honest people had fled the city. Abiel had considered leaving lest it influence his son.

The adultery and fornication that was so common in Jerusalem had caused wide-spread divorce and heartache. Families were destroyed and lives were ruined. It was no different in the palace of the king. There too was every imaginable vise.

His son Jedidiah was an obedient and loving son. Abiel couldn't have been happier with how he had turned out. But as Abiel watched Jedidiah become an adult he worried about him.

If Jedidiah were to marry one of the young girls in Jerusalem she might corrupt him. Abiel knew virtually every family in the city, and he did not know a suitable girl in any of them!

More and more his thoughts centered on what kind of girl Jedidiah would marry. He wanted to make sure that he married the right girl.

He desired to have a hand in picking his son's future bride. He did not want to leave anything to chance. So Abiel had begun to search for a suitable young woman.

There were many beautiful young ladies in Israel. Choosing a suitable bride would not be that difficult, unless of course you were picky! And Abiel was very picky.

He wasn't too concerned about their looks. He didn't care if they were rich or poor.

What he wanted to know was, *"Do they love my God? Will they love my son?"* and *"Will they be good to him and for him?"*

His business often caused Abiel to travel through the hill country of Judah. This was a poor area of small towns.

He went to Bethlehem and Hebron on a regular basis. While there he would often spend time in the markets. The market place was the best place to meet people. All people, whether they were rich or poor had to eat, and this was the place to get food.

Abiel's routine was to lean against a wall where he could watch the people as they shopped. You can tell a lot about people by the way that they treat others.

Many times he would see a beautiful maiden, only to be turned off by her attitude. He certainly did not want to have his son marry a woman who was hateful and mean.

Once in Hebron he thought that he had found the perfect girl. He began to formulate a plan to bring Jedidiah to meet her when he saw her little brothers walk up to her.

As the little boys came near anger showed on her face. With a condescending tone she insulted them, and sent them away.

"Clearly this girl is not the one for Jedidiah" thought Abiel. *"If she treats her little brothers with such contempt, she will surely treat her husband the same way!"*

The young lady never knew how close she came to marrying a good man. She ruined it by revealing what was in her heart.

Abiel began to pray harder! *"Oh Lord help me to find the right girl for my son! And please keep him from even liking the wrong girl!"*

Although he was already busy with his travelling, Abiel began to go even further away in his search. He had searched through many villages, but had not found a suitable girl.

It so happened one day that Abiel was passing through the small and poor village of **Dannah.** It was there that he spotted a beautiful young girl in the market place. He could tell that she was very hungry as she moved through the stalls, eyeing the trash for a morsel of food.

Abiel's heart went out to her. There was much suffering in Judah at that time. The policies of the king had brought great hardship on the nation.

It seemed the more ungodly the rulers turned out to be the worse the situation became. And yet they refused to repent.

This was making the poorest of the people to suffer more and more. They had no say in the policies of the kingdom, but they were the ones who paid the price.

This young girl was obviously a local girl for it seemed that everyone knew her. Abiel watched as she walked slowly past each booth, carefully checking the garbage without being too obvious.

Reaching into his bag, Abiel took out one apple. He carefully placed it down on the ground beside the last vendor's trash for this girl to find. As he leaned against the wall he also noticed a little boy walking towards the trash. He was about seven or eight, and he too was starving.

Not knowing what to do Abiel decided to let God decide who found the apple first. The boy seemed to look right at the apple, and yet he did not see it!

Then the girl found it. Carefully and somewhat slyly she picked it up. Moving away from the vendors into an alley she pulled it out where she could see it better.

Abiel felt a sense of satisfaction that she had found it, but he felt guilt that the little boy had missed out on a meal. As he reached in his bag to get another apple he saw something remarkable.

The little boy had walked up to the girl just as she had lifted her apple to eat it. Almost instantly their eyes locked. Abiel could see the conflict going on in the girl's heart for it showed in her eyes!

She was starving, and yet she wanted to give her apple to this boy. *"I wonder if she will do it?"* Abiel thought.

Abiel prayed a silent prayer, *"Oh Lord, I ask you now for a sign. If she is the one for my son, let her give that boy the apple. If she is not the one, let her keep it."*

It seemed that he had barely finished praying when he got his answer. Tenderly the girl wiped the apple with her garment she wore and handed it to the boy.

Without even a *"thank you"* the boy ran off with his prize.

As she watched him run off it seemed that her stomach ached all the more. Slowly she began the walk home. There would be no supper tonight.

Abiel followed her from a distance so as not to let her see him. He did not want to scare her. She walked a short distance and entered a small dirty looking home.

Her home had a door that was barely hanging. As she opened the door to go in it creaked and popped as if it would fall apart.

There was no light inside of the house. Apparently they could not afford oil for their lamps or even candles.

Turning back to the market Abiel began to formulate a plan; he wanted to find out about the girl but he didn't want anyone to know what he was doing. He knew that every small town was filled with constant rumors and gossiping.

He must be careful so that the girl wouldn't know what he was up to. Even if she was the one he didn't want to give the devil a chance to mess things up!

He couldn't lie, but he couldn't tell the whole truth either. So he decided to tell as much truth as necessary without being dishonest.

Walking up to the vendor's booth where he had placed his apple he said, *"I put my apple down beside your booth and a young girl picked it up. Before I could stop her she walked away with it. Do you know the girl that I am talking about?"*

"Oh yes, that would be Tamar, Loammi's daughter" said the vendor. *"She is a good girl. She must have thought that it was trash or she would never have taken it. She is not a thief I assure you sir."*

Thanking the vendor he began to walk down the row of booths. *"Tell me please, do you know the family of Loammi?"* he asked. *"Certainly we know him, what do you want to know?"* they would answer.

"Tell me about his children" Abiel would say.

"He only has a daughter and she is better than he deserves!"

It seemed that everyone had the same opinion of Tamar, and they all agreed that she was a wonderful girl.

They also all had the same opinion of her father Loammi. Everyone agreed that he was nearly useless.

They were all amazed that Tamar had turned out good. Most feared that soon Loammi would sell his daughter to one of his scoundrel friends. She was reaching maturity and if she didn't find a man to rescue her soon she would have to marry a man named Othniel, whom nobody liked.

Abiel realized that he needed to move fast. Besides, he was convinced that this was the one for Jedidiah.

"Where in all of Israel can I find a girl like this one?" he wondered. Speaking out loud he said, *"I must tell my son about her. He will surely want to meet her and her family right away."*

Chapter two: Tamar

Tamar lived in the poorest part of Judah among the foothills. The land was poor and the climate was hot. It was very hard on the farmers to scratch out a living there.

Her father and mother were among the poorest people in the village. Her father was notorious for being a drunkard, and her mother was well-known for acting sad and depressed most of the time. But everyone who knew Tamar mentioned that she was sweet and kind to others.

Her prospects in life were very limited. Unless she somehow met a wealthy young man she would spend the rest of her life poor like her parents. In fact, it was common knowledge that one of her father's friends, Othniel, had offered to take her off of his hands. It was only her mother's intervention that had saved her.

Othniel was more than twice her age and he was a widower. Tamar would inherit his children, and they were as mean as their father. It would be a miserable life and she knew it.

The thought of marrying him made Tamar feel sick every time that she thought of it. Secretly she prayed that God would help her to escape the misery that she lived in.

Tamar was tired of being hungry all of the time. She was tired of feeling hopeless. She wanted to have a future.

But there was no future in the world in which she was born. There was only poverty of mind, body and soul. It was a daily reality that she could not deny.

No one from her village had ever achieved anything notable. The unspoken belief was that no one ever would.

This hopelessness seemed to hang over her town like a cloud. It was as real as the air to her. Often she dreamed about running away somewhere, but she knew there was no place for her to go. That is the worst part about hopelessness, it shapes your thinking until you believe there is no use trying.

All that Tamar possessed were the worn out clothes that she wore. In reality all that she possessed of any value was a kind heart. But in her world that wouldn't buy her anything to eat.

Tamar's routine was to go to the market and look for scraps of vegetables or fruit that had been thrown away. Some days she would find enough to fill her stomach. Other days she found nothing.

On this particular day she had found an apple. It looked perfect! She couldn't believe her luck. As she looked it over she noticed a little boy staring at her apple!

She knew him, and he was obviously starving. Tamar's first thought was to run away with her prize! She was hungry too.

But then she felt in her heart that she should give it to him, and so she did.

Unknown to her, there was a very wealthy and important man watching all of this unfold. This man had the ability to change her life forever. She couldn't have imagined how important this moment was.

As she watched the little boy run away eating her apple she thought, *"He didn't even say thanks!"*

Then she felt even sadder. She was used to going hungry, but to have had a meal and then to not have it! Now she was even hungrier than if she had not seen the apple!

Slowly she walked home. Her eyes never looked up nor did she look behind her. If she had looked back she would have seen that a man was following her.

But Tamar wasn't paying attention to anything. She was just tired and hungry and tired of being hungry.

As the sun was setting she fought back the tears that were already forming in her eyes. The only word that could have described her feelings was "miserable!"

As she entered her home she noticed her father was slumped over the table. He was apparently drunk again! Even though they didn't have any money for food he somehow managed to find money for wine.

Hearing her come in to the house, he roused himself a bit. Turning towards the door, it took him a minute to focus on who had come in. Tamar recoiled when she looked in his eyes; they were unusually red and puffy. She thought he looked angry. He usually became mean when he got drunk, and the more that he drank the meaner he got.

"Tamar!" he bellowed.

"Yes father" Tamar replied.

"Tomorrow you are to go work in farmer Othniel's field."

Tamar's heart sunk! Othniel was the man who kept asking to marry her. Obviously her father had promised to send her to work for Othniel in exchange for some wine. Othniel knew Loammi's weakness.

Tamar wanted to rebel against her father, but what could she say? There was no chance of her disobeying her father. So she replied that she would go, but she did it in such a way that her father could tell she was unhappy. If he noticed her mood he didn't show it. He just turned his head away from her and slipped back into his stupor.

That night Tamar found it very hard to sleep. As she lay in bed she prayed and cried to God.

"Please don't let me be married off to someone like Othniel Lord! If you help me I will serve you forever, but please don't allow that man to become my husband! I would rather die than to be married to someone like him!"

Tamar seldom prayed, and when she did she was always trying to force God to make a deal with her. She didn't know God in a personal way.

Sometime during the night she drifted off to sleep.

Awaking the next morning she noticed that the sun wasn't shining. *"Maybe it will rain today and I won't have to go to Othniel's"* she thought. But it didn't rain that day.

Walking into the main room she looked towards her mother Tirzah. *"Mother, I am to go work in Othniel's fields today"* she said.

"Yes I know" her mother replied without looking at her. Tamar's mother was not a happy person to be around. She was chronically depressed about her life. She rarely thought about anyone else's problems but her own.

It had been Tamar's last hope that her mother would stop her from having to go to Othniel's. But she either didn't care, or else she had no choice in the matter.

Slowly Tamar walked out into the street and made her way to Othniel's. As she approached him, Othniel smiled at her. He was trying hard to make her like him, but it wasn't working. Tamar felt nothing but anger every time she looked at him. His wife had died, and left him to raise their three boys. The boys were becoming as cruel as their father.

"I am so happy to see you again my dear" he said, *"please make yourself at home!"*

Tamar just ignored him. *"What do you want me to do today?"* she asked.

Realizing that Tamar was angry only made Othniel even more hateful than usual.

Crossing his arms as a sign that he was mad, he said to her, *"You can pick up rocks out of my field and carry them to the edges. If you do a good job I will feed you, if not I won't give you anything! Your father owes me money so I don't owe you anything!"*

His children laughed when he spoke to Tamar. They enjoyed watching their father torment her.

Throughout that long day Tamar picked rocks out of Othniel's field. About midday he gave her some stale bread and water. That was the first meal she had had in two days, but she hated to eat it in front of him.

It was all so humiliating! Othniel's field was on the main road into town and everyone who passed by laughed at her. Several of her "friends" asked her if she had married Othniel, thinking it was funny.

As much as she hated Othniel, she was beginning to hate her father even more. If she thought it was possible she would have run away. That way he would not get a dowry for her, and maybe then he would actually go to work!

But Tamar knew that she had nowhere to run. To run away from home was dangerous. Young girls were not safe travelling alone because there were bandits on the main roads. She was too weak from hunger to make it very far anyway.

So she just kept working picking up rocks as the day continued to drag on.

Finally the sun began to set and Othniel told her she could go home. His boys taunted her and called her names as she left, but she did her best to ignore them.

Slowly the dirty and sweaty girl walked home, never realizing that her life was about to change for the better. All that she thought of was a way to commit suicide without going to hell. She knew that there was no way.

Feeling as if the entire town was laughing at her, all she could do was cry and pray.

Chapter three: Abiel tells Jedidiah

Abiel arrived home early in the morning. He was exhausted from travelling all night, but he wouldn't rest until he had spoken to his son.

As he entered his home he saw that his son was already busy doing his chores.

How he loved this boy! He never complained about his work. He knew Jedidiah was lonely at times. All of his friends had long since married but Jedidiah was still single.

Sometimes he would tell his father how a friend had teased him about not being married. But Jedidiah was not going to rush into a marriage just because his friends did.

He would tell them all the same thing, *"When I marry it will be because I love my wife, not because I am tired of being lonely!"*

Walking towards his son, Abiel felt as if he would burst if he didn't tell him his good news;

"Jedidiah, I have found the perfect bride for you! She is beautiful and she is the sweetest girl I have ever seen. You must come and meet her."

Jedidiah was shocked and overjoyed at the same time.

"What is she like?" he asked. *"Where does she live?"*

Then he finally asked, *"And what is her name?"*

Laughing, Abiel began to fill Jedidiah in on the details.

"Her name is Tamar, but don't hold that against her son" he said.

He said this because Tamar was an infamous name in Israel.

There had been two notable women in the scriptures by that name, and both of them had terrible things happen to them.

The first woman named Tamar had been Judah's daughter-in-law. She was married to Judah's oldest son but he died before having any children.

Judah forced his second son to marry Tamar but he too died before they had children. She should have been married then to Judah's youngest son, but he refused to give her to him.

A married woman whose husband had died was under the control of her father in law. Only he had the right to decide who she would marry if his son died.

Judah blamed Tamar for his other boys dying. His two sons had been evil men, but Tamar had to bear the shame. Everyone acted as if she was bad luck. To protect his youngest son he sent her home to live with her father. Then he pretended she no longer existed.

Years later Tamar realized that Judah was never going to allow her to marry his youngest son so she came up with a plan. She disguised herself to her father-in-law so that he wouldn't recognize her. Then she convinced him that she was a prostitute.

Not knowing that it was Tamar, he had sex with her that night and left before daylight. He never realized who the woman was that he had slept with.

Tamar went back home to her father's house but soon it became evident that she was pregnant.

When Judah heard that she was pregnant he demanded that she be killed.

But Tamar had cleverly taken Judah's signet ring and staff the night she was with him. When she was brought before him she held them up saying, *"By the man who owns this am I pregnant."*

Judah was shocked! He hadn't recognized Tamar in the darkness. There was nothing for him to do but let her come and live with him. He did not take her as a wife but he wanted to be with the child she bore.

Tamar had twin boys named Pharez and Zarah. Her two boys grew to become the greatest men in the tribe of Judah. Nearly every man in the tribe was a descendent of one of Tamar's sons.

The second woman named Tamar was King David's daughter. She was a beautiful girl who was raped by her half-brother Amnon.

Amnon loved her so much that he stopped eating. Not knowing the real reason why his son was so sickly, David sent Tamar to cook Amnon some food.

Instead of eating the food, Amnon grabbed Tamar and forcibly raped her. Suddenly, instead of loving her he hated her.

Every time that he thought of her he was forced to think of what an awful thing that he had done to her.

Amnon was only Tamar's half-brother. Her full brother's name was Absalom. He brought her to his home to live as a widow the rest of her life. He eventually killed Amnon for what he did to Tamar.

This set off a chain of events that would lead to a revolution in Israel and the death of Absalom and thousands of others.

The name of Tamar became a synonym for bad luck. Tamar often wondered why her parents would have chosen to name her what they did.

The children in her hometown mocked her because of her name. But Abiel and Jedidiah weren't too concerned about her name.

"She is beautiful son. She will make you a fine wife and will make a wonderful daughter to me."

Abiel's wife had died while giving birth to Jedidiah, and he had never remarried. If his wife had lived he had hoped their second child would be a daughter. He realized now that his only hope of having a daughter was a daughter in law. Jedidiah's wife would be his daughter.

The thought of getting married had filled Jedidiah's thoughts for a long time. He had longed for the love and companionship that marriage brought. He too had been looking for a potential bride, but he had not found one that he thought his father would approve of.

Jedidiah knew that his father was very protective of him. Abiel would never pick a girl unless he was sure that she was the one!

This process of picking a bride was called **the Shiddukhin**.

Although Abiel had great influence over his son, Jedidiah's consent was needed. If Jedidiah was not happy with his father's choice he was free to say no. Also the bride and her family must agree to the marriage.

Abiel would send Jedidiah's best friend named **Ha-Melitz** to meet with the father of Tamar. He was charged with negotiating the bride-price which was called **the Mohar.**

It was customary for the groom's father to pay a dowry to the bride's family. Both sides would decide what the dowry was and until it was paid the courtship could not begin. This was the Mohar.

Although the father of the bride received the Mohar, the bride also had a price. Her price was called **the Mattan.**

The Mattan was considered a love gift. This was how the groom would show his love for his bride to be. His gifts were meant to set her free from relying on her family for support.

The Mattan also were **gifts of excess**. The groom would give her more than she needed as proof that his love for her was a love in excess.

The groom would not be allowed to be alone with his bride to be. Jedidiah would have to make an appointment to see Tamar and even then they could not talk in private. Everything had to be open and above board so that there would not be the slightest hint of scandal.

His best friend would make certain she had everything that she needed. This friend's only desire was to see that Jedidiah and Tamar would become a happily married couple.

Jedidiah had one friend that he could trust with such an important job, and that was Ha-Melitz.

Jedidiah knew that no matter what Tamar would need Ha-Melitz would make sure she had it. Everything that Abiel possessed would be at her disposal. Ha-Melitz would see to it that Tamar did not lack.

So father and son agreed to send Ha-Melitz to start negotiations with Tamar's family.

As he rode into Dannah the evening sun was sinking on the horizon. The town did not impress him in the least. It was worse than poor; it was ugly! And the people all had a hard look to them. As he surveyed the market area he wondered what had made Abiel think to look here for a wife.

The wind was blowing fairly strong from the south, and it was coming off of the desert. The result was a hot dose of sand hitting him in the face as he rode.

Abiel had given him precise directions on how to find Tamar's house, and he went right to it. Ha-Melitz slowly got off of his horse and walked to the door.

It was as pitiful a house as he had ever seen. Inwardly he wondered what kind of people lived behind that door. Reaching out his hand he knocked.

Tamar's father came to the door and opened it slightly, not knowing why such a well-dressed man would visit.

"And who may I ask are you?" he snorted. Apparently he thought it was someone coming to collect on a debt.

Tamar was frightened by his arrival at their home. She had seen Ha-Melitz standing in the doorway and chose to hide. Her clothing was unsightly and she was dirty from working in the field. There was no way that she wanted anyone respectable to see her looking like she did!

"I represent Abiel of Jerusalem" said Ha-Melitz, *"He would like to speak to you about your daughter Tamar. Could he and his son Jedidiah come and sit with you to discuss the possibility of a union between Jedidiah and Tamar?"*

Loammi just stared at Ha-Melitz without saying a word. He didn't comprehend what Ha-Melitz said.

It never occurred to him that anyone respectable would want to marry Tamar. When he heard Ha-Melitz ask his question he thought he must have heard him wrong.

"Please say that again. I'm not sure I heard you right" he said.

Once again Ha-Melitz spoke the same words.

Loammi and his wife stood silently looking at the stranger!

Ha-Melitz wasn't sure what to say or do now. They just stared at him as if he had spoken gibberish!

Finally Tamar's mother spoke, *"You mean, someone from Jerusalem wants to marry **our daughter**? Why?"*

This was becoming increasingly bizarre to Ha-Melitz, and he wasn't sure what to say now.

"His father Abiel was in your village two days ago. He saw your beautiful daughter in the market place. He is very particular about his son, and I am sure he would never have picked Tamar unless he was certain about his choice" he answered.

Loammi stared at him for a minute, and then he finally realized the magnitude of the moment.

He was very happy to hear that such an illustrious family as the family of Abiel was interested in his daughter. That meant that he would receive the Mohar and he could certainly use the money!

"We would be honored to meet with your worthy master and his son at his convenience" he said.

Ha-Melitz then set a time for the meeting and left for Jerusalem. After he mounted his horse and began to ride away Tamar came out from where she was hiding. Holding on to her mother's arm she just stared at the man riding his horse out of town.

For several minutes the little family stood in the doorway and stared blankly into each other's eyes. All of them seemed to be asking themselves the same question, *"What just happened?"*

It was only after Tamar stepped out into the street to watch Ha-Melitz ride off that she began to grasp what was going on- she was about to get married! Turning back towards the doorway she stared at her parents in amazement. And then it hit them all at the same time; they had a lot of work to do!

Tamar and her parents spent the rest of that night cleaning their house. Then early the next morning they started getting everything ready for the evening guests. There was so much to do if they were to make their house presentable! They obviously didn't have the things that they needed so they would have to beg or borrow to get them.

In those days the men would recline on cushions while the women served. It was customary for the bride's family to serve the meal. Of course if the family was poor, the meal would be simple.

Tamar's family had few cushions and no food. Her father had to promise the vendors at the market that he would repay them from the Mohar. They first said no to his request. But after he informed them that Abiel of Jerusalem was the one who was coming they agreed. They trusted Abiel, but nobody trusted Loammi.

Loammi would have to have vegetables and fruit as well as new wine to drink. If he failed to provide the basic meal there would be no contract. Not to mention that it would be insulting to Abiel.

Somehow Tamar's father was able to beg or borrow enough to make a presentable meal for Abiel and Jedidiah.

Her father was so excited that he was acting ridiculous!

"He is rich Tamar!" he said. *"You will be rich! You can help us! Just think of what it will be like for you to live in Jerusalem, and we can live with you!"*

That last part caused Tamar to shudder; she would like to rid herself of her father and mother. And as far as being rich, Tamar thought that meant having decent clothes to wear and food to eat was rich.

And as far as living with the society crowd in Jerusalem she didn't have the slightest idea of what that meant.

She began to worry. Would she know how to act? She wasn't educated. How would she be able to carry on a decent conversation with her new husband and his family? What if he had friends over? Her knowledge in life was all wrapped up in a small village. Would she fit in?

For Tamar it seemed as if that day lasted forever. She had barely slept. Every time she closed her eyes her mind would start racing! Doubt and fear were mixed with joy and hope. She only hoped that something didn't go wrong. Quietly she prayed that God would help her. She knew that this was her one chance in life. There may never be another.

As the sun began to sink on the horizon, Tamar's heart began to beat faster. *"Soon"* she kept saying, *"Soon!"*

It was nearly sunset when Abiel, Jedidiah and Ha-Melitz approached Tamar's house. With a polite knock on the door Abiel announced their arrival. Quickly Tamar's father opened the door and the family bowed in honor.

Normally such important people would not enter such a humble home. This was an honor for the whole village, and every house had eyes peering out of the windows and doors.

It seems that there are always jealous and envious people who resent seeing someone else get blessed. They can't seem to keep from saying negative things. It was the same in Tamar's village.

"Abiel will change his mind when he sees who she really is!" one woman had boasted.

"I would love to hear his thoughts when he sees the inside of their house!" laughed another.

Others were more insulting than that, *"She's too dumb for an intelligent boy to marry. Abiel's son must have something wrong with him."*

Not many in that little village could conceive in their small imaginations that Jedidiah, being of sound mind, could love Tamar. Nor could they fathom the thought that a poor girl from Dannah could find happiness.

Tamar knew that her "friends" would think such things. She had thought some of the very same things about herself. In her heart she knew that what was happening was beyond her.

She might as well have been transported to a different planet as to go to Jerusalem, the city of the king.

Jerusalem was a world unto itself. Everything about it was different than her world. Once she and Jedidiah were married she would have to force herself to talk to people, and she didn't have the slightest idea of what they would talk about! In her world she was excited to find an apple! What on earth do they discuss in Jerusalem?

All of these doubts and fears made her almost unable to walk! She was nearly paralyzed by fear.

It was more than she could bear, and yet she had imagined this very scenario so many times; a young and handsome Prince Charming would come and rescue her from her depressing life. But that was only a dream; this was real!

She could choose what happened in her imagination. But life was not under her control. In fact, she felt as if it were spinning out of control. Yet she wanted this! It was a dream come true.

As she was trying to calm herself down, she heard the noise of approaching horses on the dirt road.

As she listened she could hear the horses stop outside of her house, and the sound of footsteps coming closer.

Then she heard the knock on her door! In her heart she wanted to run to the door, and simultaneously run out the back door! Fortunately for her she did neither.

Chapter four: The lovers meet

Tamar's home was small and the door was low. As Loammi bowed gracefully and backed away from the entry, Abiel stepped through. As Abiel entered the house he said, *"Shalom to this house"* and they replied, *"And Shalom to you and yours."*

Jedidiah stepped in slowly. It took him a moment for his eyes to adjust to the low light inside of the house.

Suddenly his eyes met Tamar's at the same moment that she looked at him. It was truly love at first sight!

Tamar's heart seemed to stop for a moment when she locked eyes with Jedidiah. He was tall and handsome, with a look of authority that calmed her fears. He was more than she had ever imagined in a husband.

For a few seconds she neither breathed nor thought. Everything in her wanted to run into his arms. She knew that he was the one for her. Fears and doubts seemed to disappear in a moment, and suddenly she no longer doubted.

Jedidiah also felt his heart skip. The feelings that he had felt were more about pleasing his father. He only hoped Tamar would be worth the trip. But after seeing her he completely forgot about Abiel.

There is a quality that women possess that most men do not; and that is the ability to speak with just their eyes. As Jedidiah stared into Tamar's eyes he could see that she was happy to see him. Tamar's eyes gave Jedidiah confidence. In her eyes he saw love and joy.

Slowly it occurred to both Tamar and Jedidiah that they were being spoken to! Abiel had said something to her, but she had not heard him. Tamar's father told her to stand straight and present herself to Abiel.

She felt a blush come over her as she realized she had been quite rude to her future father-in-law. But Abiel just laughed. He had spied the two when they locked eyes, and he saw that they were very happy already. That is what he had wanted.

Standing quite straight and proper she apologized to Abiel, and bowed her head. But he assured her that an apology was not necessary.

Normally Loammi was not eloquent, but this day he outdid himself by saying,

"It is with great joy that we welcome such distinguished guests into our home. Shalom and God's peace be to you and your distinguished household. It is with humble gratitude that we thank you for the honor of having you here. Please be seated around our humble table."

"It is we who are honored to be here" replied Abiel.

As the evening progressed the conversation flowed easily from one subject to another. Finally the time came to get down to business.

"My dear friend Loammi, I first noticed your lovely daughter in the market place. I watched her as she gave a hungry boy her apple" said Abiel. He did not mention anything that might have caused either embarrassment or shame to Tamar or her family. It was not necessary to mention that he knew that she was hungry and poor.

"I could see the love of God was in her. As I was praying silently, it seemed to me that God said "Yes, she is the one you have been seeking."

"If I may be so forward, are you and the damsel in agreement to allow my son Jedidiah to be her betrothed?"

"I am, and I believe from my daughter's expression on her face, she is too!" said Loammi. *"Are you willing my daughter?"*

"I am willing" said Tamar.

"May I be your servant my Lord" she said to Jedidiah as she again bowed her head in submission.

The next few minutes were spent in determining the Mohar and the Mattan.

"Do you accept my son's offer of the Mohar?" Abiel asked.

"We do accept" Tamar's father answered.

Actually he was overjoyed! They were offering much more of a Mohar than Othniel was willing to pay him for Tamar.

When all parties were satisfied Jedidiah was allowed to speak to Tamar. For the first time he was allowed to touch her. He was not supposed to touch her again until their wedding night.

Taking her by the hand, he stared intently into her eyes and said *"Be thou my wife according to the Law of Moses and of Israel."*

"I will be your wife, and you will be my husband forever, according to the Law of Moses and of Israel" she answered.

And with that single touch and simple statement they were now considered husband and wife.

The rules of the marriage ceremony were very strict and they had to be written down. In this contract the Mohar was made clear.

Also the rights of the bride were spelled out. To protect the woman from being mistreated in any way, all of her rights were written in detail.

She could return home to her father at any time in the marriage if her husband failed to meet his obligations.

The groom also made promises of support that were written down. This was the Mattan. He promised not only to love and care for her once they were wed, but also to provide for her until the day of the wedding.

This contract was called **the Ketubbah.**

Ha-Melitz carefully wrote the rules of the Ketubbah.

It began with the words, *"You are hereby betrothed unto me according to the Law of Moses and of Israel."* Then their names were added as well as the family's names.

"Jedidiah, son of Abiel of the family Judah said to this maiden daughter of the family of Loammi, "Be thou my wife according to the Law of Moses and Israel, Amen" wrote Ha-Melitz.

There was one more ritual that had to be performed before it was legal and binding and it was called **the Kiddushin toast.**

The Kiddushin is a marriage toast. This was done with new wine because old or fermented wine signified rot, and was considered as an insult.

Loammi had been fortunate that the grapes were just ripening at the time he needed new wine.

As host it was his duty to honor his guest first, so the privilege of presenting the first blessing went to Abiel.

With moist eyes Abiel raised his cup and said slowly, *"My greatest wish for you both is that your love will grow so strong through the years that you will look back on this day as the day that you loved each other the least!"*

There was no way that he could have known how prophetic his words were that night.

Next Jedidiah raised his cup and spoke. His voice too was choked with emotion as he said, *"I wish to convey to the parents of my lovely bride my heartfelt thanks for raising such a beautiful daughter. I promise to honor you by loving her. From this day forward you shall also be parents unto me, and I thank you again from the bottom of my heart!"*

Loammi then spoke, *"May these early years of your new life be filled with joy. May your later years be filled with happiness, and may you never live one moment in regret. Live your lives together as God meant for you to. Love greatly! Please God and you will always please your parents!"*

They then partook of the juice and proclaimed *"Shalom"* again.

Jedidiah spoke to Tamar once more before he left. He said, *"In my father's house there are many rooms. I go to prepare a Chador for you. When my father says that it is time I will return for you, and take you to my home."*

The Chador is the honeymoon chamber. It is not just a bedroom with a bed. It contains the honeymoon bed, but it is far more. Jedidiah would have it ready for Tamar by making it something that Tamar would love. He would spend the time finding out her likes and dislikes so that he could make it perfect for her.

"I will be waiting and I will be ready" said Tamar.

All too soon it seemed it was time for Abiel and Jedidiah to return to Jerusalem.

Ha-Melitz inquired about a place to lodge nearby so he could perform the duty of the best-man.

Loammi had no extra space, but he said that just down the street there was a room for rent. Ha-Melitz would need to be near in case Tamar required anything. Abiel provided Ha-Melitz with more than enough money to meet his and Tamar's needs, and then they went out into the night.

It was getting late. While it seemed to Jedidiah that they had only been at Tamar's house a short while, they had actually been there for over three hours.

As Jedidiah looked heavenward he thought of how blessed he was. Quietly he whispered, *"Thank you God! Thank you!"* He had known that his father was trying to find him a bride. He had been quite worried about what kind of girl his father would find. Now he was relieved. Tamar was perfect.

Abiel was also thankful to God, but his eyes were busy surveying the town. It seemed to him that every door was cracked just enough so that someone could peer out. He thought about the people of this little village. Many of them were born here and most likely would die here. Most had never ventured more than a few miles from their homes. This was the biggest thing to happen in their life-times.

As they rode slowly out of town Jedidiah too began to notice that they were being watched. He wondered if they could tell how happy he was.

The next morning Tamar woke up late. Normally she would have been up before dawn, helping her mother Tirzah prepare their meager breakfast. But this day she slept past breakfast.

Tamar had been so tired and relieved when she went to bed that she fell to sleep almost immediately. The stress of the previous day had taken its toll on her.

When she came into the main room she was surprised to see that there was plenty of food on their table. What was even more surprising to her was that her mother was smiling. Tamar hadn't seen her mother smile in such a long time that she was momentarily shocked when she did.

Her father was also happy as he walked through the village. He was behaving as if he were a rich man. He was not wasting any time spending the Mohar!

Tamar wanted to speak to her father, but he was nowhere to be found. He was busy telling everyone he could about the previous night's events. Even the harshest critics in town were impressed.

It was hard to deny that God had surely blessed Loammi's family. The thing that puzzled his neighbors was why was he blessed? More than one wondered aloud why God would do anything for Loammi.

Strangely it seemed that she was out of place in her own home. Everything was different. She was different! She was now married to Jedidiah Ben Abiel! From this day forward she was his wife and he was her husband.

The courtship of a couple in old Israel was very different than what westerners are used to. Although the couple was considered married, they would not even kiss until the wedding night. All things had to be done properly.

After eating breakfast, Tamar tried on a new outfit that Abiel had brought for her. For the first time in her memory she walked into town clean, her stomach was full and she had a new outfit on!

As she looked at the people's faces she realized that almost all of them were smiling at her.

Not all of course. Othniel wasn't happy.

He just gave her a dirty look. And his kids stuck their tongues out at her. Tamar laughed at them, she couldn't help herself! Just the thought of almost being the step-mother of those little monsters scared her. But now she knew that it would never happen. The joy of that thought caused her to laugh out loud.

It didn't take her long to realize that she was the most popular person in the village. Even the most critical people admitted that Tamar was blessed; they just couldn't understand why she was, and truthfully, neither could she.

Chapter five: Dannah

Dannah was typical of the many small towns in southern Judah in those days. It had nothing valuable in it, and there really was no reason to visit it.

The name *"Dannah"* means *"He will judge."*

It was rumored that it was named Dannah by a Judge of Israel. Hundreds of years before, the people believed, the judge cursed their town, and it was his fault they were so miserable.

In reality that was not what happened, but sometimes a story takes on a life of its own. The truth was the name had nothing to do with a curse. It was named Dannah as a promise that God would judge justly.

Over the years the false story became reality for Dannah's citizens. As one generation after another believed it, it became a fact in their minds. They just could not conceive of success coming their way.

For Tamar and the people of Dannah, hopelessness had become a belief system. It was unspoken, but it was deep felt and tangible. They truly believed that they were not destined to succeed in life.

There were numerous stories in that small town of people who had tried to get ahead only to fail miserably. One young man married a girl from another town whose father was a wealthy merchant. It seemed that he had broken the curse. But unfortunately he did not.

After several months of living the life of a successful merchant he began to drink and cheat on his new bride. Their marriage lasted less than a year before her father stepped in and sent him home.

What none of them seemed to realize was that their plight was actually a self-fulfilling prophecy. Each one who had failed had brought their misery on themselves. It was as if deep down inside they knew that they were out of their element. On an unconscious level they worked to sabotage their new life in order to return to what they were comfortable with.

Mentally and spiritually they were incapable of accepting success just as some people in life are incapable of accepting defeat. The people of Dannah hated their lives; in fact they daily bemoaned their plight! But it was what they were used to, no matter how miserable they were.

This attitude was as evident in what they did not say as much as it was in what they did say. It affected every detail of their lives from the way that they prayed to what they dreamed of.

Tamar dreamed of living in a large spacious palace, but in her heart she feared such a reality. If she ever thought about how she would have to entertain guests it scared her. She refused to think too deeply about it because she knew it was beyond her abilities.

For Jedidiah and Abiel, Tamar was a sweet and pretty girl. They were not aware of how she thought. They could only guess by what they saw with their eyes. However, Tamar had more faith in the belief that she would fail than she did in what reality told her.

There was no reason why she couldn't succeed in life. But she firmly believed that there were people that God favored, and He made sure that they succeeded. And then there were people like the ones in her village that He did not favor.

For Tamar and her townsfolk, everything bad that happened was someone else's fault. Rich people usually got the blame, although God received plenty of blame too. No matter what scriptures were quoted to them saying otherwise, they believed what they believed.

This inward belief system would soon sabotage Tamar's life in ways that no one could imagine. Unfortunately, there was nothing that Jedidiah or Abiel could have done differently to stop it.

That was why the people of her village could not accept that Tamar would be happy; nobody from Dannah could be happy!

Tamar could feel the doubt surrounding her as she walked. But there were also reasons for optimism this day.

Tamar was the most popular and successful person to ever come from Dannah! And her good fortune was less than a day old!

The second most popular person was Jedidiah's friend Ha-Melitz. His name meant "Comforter" and he was well named, for he was a source of comfort to Abiel and his son. There were many people in Dannah that vied for his attention, but he refused to be distracted. He was only concerned about making sure his friend's marriage was a success.

He had much work to do before the wedding day. He would be spending his time instructing Tamar on what Jedidiah was like, what his interest were and what was expected of her when she became his wife. Tamar had been lifted from obscurity and ignorance in a day. Now, much would be required of her.

Tamar thought that becoming a wife meant that she could behave as her mother did. This was not going to be possible for her as Jedidiah's wife. Her mother stayed hidden at home most of the time. She seemed to live in the shadows.

Her mother Tirzah just existed, but she really didn't know how to live. She seemed to always be chronically depressed or disinterested. She seldom smiled and never laughed.

As Jedidiah's wife and Abiel's daughter in law, Tamar would not be able to act like her mother did. Everyone knew who they were, and so everyone would know who Tamar was.

This truth was a little hard for Tamar to come to grips with. She wanted to marry Jedidiah, but she didn't feel adequate. Ha-Melitz was going to do everything in his power to make her ready.

He knew that he had to make Tamar see the necessity of improving herself. It was going to take a lot of work.

The betrothal time was called **the Kiddushin.** This was the time that the groom proved his wife. If she was not true to him he could divorce her, and if he was not true to her she could divorce him.

It was during this time that the bride and groom would fast and pray. It was a very solemn time and they would seek to be sanctified from all filthiness of the flesh. Godliness was the goal of their lives.

The bride would also partake of a ceremonial baptism called **the Mikveh**. Only the bride partook of this act of sanctification. She did this in the presence of qualified witnesses including her mother. It was her way of proving that she belonged completely and only to her husband.

In ancient times it was considered wise to wait at least a year from the proposal to the consummation of the marriage. This would give the couple time to really get to know each other.

Although they were not allowed to touch each other, they would be allowed to visit as long as they were in the company of her parents.

Jews believed that all marriages were ordained of God so God had to be included in every detail of the courtship. Nothing was done that would cause God displeasure. More than anything they would need His favor and blessing on their lives.

It was for this reason that they waited so long. They had to please God first! For the Jews the marriage represented a new home, a new start and a new life.

Jedidiah had to do everything right and each thing that he did represented something sacred to the Jews.

Jedidiah's main task was to prepare **a Chador.** This was a bed-chamber where he and Tamar would live in his father's house. This was the special room designed specifically for Tamar.

Everything must be perfect for the bride. Her wants and desires were important to the design of the Chador. This would be one of the proofs of the grooms love for his bride. If he messed the Chador up, he would never get a second chance. He must do this right.

He first cleaned out a room that was sufficient in size. His father had plenty of rooms but this was the one his bride and he would call home. Then he began to prepare it special for Tamar.

He found out what she liked most, and what she didn't like. Nothing could be left to chance. The Chador must be exactly perfect for Tamar.

Next he began the work on **the Huppah** canopy. The Huppah was erected outside under the open sky. This was to symbolize to God that nothing was hidden from Him, and that He was a witness to their vows.

The Huppah was a decorated cloth that was about five feet six inches by three feet nine inches. It was made especially for the couple and would have their names embroidered on it.

It was held up by four posts. This too was symbolic. When God and the two angels came to visit Abraham it is said that his tent was open on all four sides.

The four posts represent the hospitality that Abraham gave to God, and that the new couple would also give to God.

The couple would stand under the Huppah canopy as they took their vows before God. This meant that their marriage was divinely blessed and ordained. The Huppah was erected to signify that the ceremony and institution of marriage has divine origins.

It was in the first book of the Old Testament that God instituted the marriage covenant. It was in the last book of the Old Testament that he condemned men for breaking the marriage covenant with their wives.

If there is one thing that the Jews believe in, it is a covenant! To the Jews, a covenant was a matter of life and death. It was an eternal contract between the people and God. So no one wanted to make a covenant unless they were confident that they could keep it. And, no one ever wished to break a covenant, because then they angered God.

This was serious work, and it would keep Jedidiah very busy. The Huppah canopy could not be mass-produced; it had to be made by hand. It would represent the character of both bride and groom.

The Chador had to be perfect. It was to be proof that the groom was careful and considerate of the bride's wishes. Therefore it had to be flawless so the bride would be happy with the effort that he put into it.

Jedidiah had many friends and neighbors in Jerusalem, and all of them wanted to know when his wedding would be. In olden times the groom had an answer for all such inquiries,

"No man knows the day or the hour. Only my father knows"

This was his answer to all who asked him the day. It was also the answer that Tamar was to give to those who asked her,

"No man knows the day or the hour, only my husband's father knows. He will decide when it is time. Until then, we must be ready!"

Abiel would also be busy preparing for the wedding feast. Abiel was actually the one who decided when everything was perfect, and he was the master of the feast.

Once he was satisfied that all things were complete and ready he would tell Jedidiah to go take his bride. But until he was satisfied, Jedidiah and Tamar would have to patiently wait.

For Tamar this time was precious. She needed to spend it learning how to be a good wife and mother. Ha-Melitz was her constant source of information. He came from Abiel's home, and knew everything about it.

She would have to learn how to live in his world, and this became her biggest hurdle.

Tamar also was going to be occupied. Her closest friends would have to be made aware of the coming wedding day. Although no one knew when Jedidiah would come, they had to be ready.

Every Jewish girl knew better than to be late for a wedding. Once the doors were shut they could not get in. There would be no wedding crashers.

Tamar also had to prepare her wedding gown. This would not have been like what brides wear today, but would have to be hand-made.

Most young girls in her village wore simple gowns made from common cloth. But Tamar's would be special. Ha-Melitz assured Tamar that hers would be of the highest quality befitting the bride of Jedidiah.

Over the next few months Ha-Melitz would be busy also. He was the liaison between Jedidiah and Tamar. It was his job to convey to Jedidiah what Tamar needed. He also had to get Tamar ready and to keep her ready.

Keeping a young girl prepared was quite a challenge for Ha-Melitz. Once the initial euphoria wore off, she seemed to get bored with waiting. He was constantly speaking to her that she must live ready.

It was obvious to Ha-Melitz that though Tamar had a good heart, she knew almost nothing about being a good wife. Her own mother was a poor example. Tamar would need to pay attention to what Ha-Melitz taught her.

It was also obvious to him that she wasn't very teachable. The lazy example that her parents showed her was proving to be a detriment to her learning.

"Why do I have to?" seemed to be her favorite phrase.

"Because it is what your husband asks of you!" was his constant reminder.

"What is asked of you is not hard or impossible to do. It is no more than anyone would ask of their bride. This is for your good and for your happiness. Jedidiah has chosen you. His father chose you. You have been greatly honored; you should want to please them for choosing you" he told her one day.

It was clear to Ha-Melitz that Tamar seemed to think that she was already perfect enough.

Many times Ha-Melitz would have to remind her of the love that Jedidiah had for her. It seemed to him that she forgot how much he loved her every time something went wrong.

"Child, don't you understand that this is for your good?" he would say. *"Your happiness is important to me, to Abiel your father-in-law and to your husband."*

"I know, I know. So you have told me. But if I was good enough when he chose me, why should I have to change now?" she replied to him.

Ha-Melitz also soon realized that Tamar was getting bad advice from her friends and family. They had never improved their lot in life, and yet they were giving advice! He worked hard to convince her that her life would be better in Jerusalem in Jedidiah's house. He pointed out the failings of the advisor's she was listening to. But Tamar seemed to be ignoring most of what he said.

The gifts that she had received made her extremely happy for a while, but she seemed to become bored with them very quickly.

She asked Ha-Melitz if her husband would give her more gifts. She still hadn't used everything that he had given her before, but she was greedily asking for more!

This tendency was dangerous and Ha-Melitz knew it. He dealt with it head-on in a conversation with Tamar, but she got mad at him and stormed off.

Tamar knew that her husband would come for her eventually, but she wanted him to come now! Not later. She hated Dannah and she wanted to leave it immediately.

After spending her life without hope of a future she suddenly had hope. But she hated having to wait for it. It was clear to Ha-Melitz that Tamar needed to learn patience!

The first month of her engagement she did splendid. She took everything to heart that Ha-Melitz taught her.

But the second month she began to lose her enthusiasm. The euphoria that she had at the beginning was gone, and now she seemed to view life as dull and boring again.

By the sixth month of her engagement she was becoming noticeably irritable. Ha-Melitz's work was becoming burdensome.

It seemed that everything that he tried to get her to do was met with hostility. When he mentioned anything that she needed to do she became angry at him.

"Now what do I have to change?" Tamar seemed to spit the words out at him.

He replied, *"Do you not love your husband?"*

"What do you mean? Of course I do! Why would you ask me that?" she retorted angrily.

"If you love him as you say, then doing what will make him happy should not be burdensome to you." Ha-Melitz calmly replied. *"Love is all the reason you need for becoming the bride he deserves."*

The thought of moving to Jedidiah's home was actually frightening to Tamar. More than anything she wanted to escape from her world and be a part of his. But she doubted that she would fit in.

Secretly she wished that she could run away to a quiet little place where no one would ask anything of her.

The time had gone by far too slow for Tamar. It seemed to her that her wedding day might never come. Her friends were always telling her about a girl just like her whose husband never came. It seemed they always had a bad story to tell her. These friends of hers were becoming a very bad influence.

The constant waiting and being told to be ready were becoming tiresome. In many ways Tamar was spoiled.

Most people think that only rich people are spoiled but that is not true. Many people become spoiled because they are so selfish. One does not have to possess much to be selfish.

Tamar was spoiled to being able to whine and complain any time she wished. She was used to pouting when she didn't get her way or when she was angry. This pouty behavior had become part of her personality. She was so used to living life this way that she never considered it as wrong.

She had not learned to trust God with her problems. She didn't vocalize it, but her attitude revealed her thoughts.

Patience was the thing she lacked most. Although God had already blessed her tremendously, she quietly grumbled because she was forced to wait so long.

This sort of trivial behavior makes a person miss some of God's greatest gifts in life. Things like a beautiful sunrise or a full stomach soon are not appreciated. They are lost to us because we have lost our ability to be thankful.

Chapter six: Tamar is unfaithful

Tamar had never felt good about herself. Her home had no mirrors for her to preen in front of. She did not have nice clothes to show off. Her father was a constant source of embarrassment for her, and she usually was dirty.

Because she thought so little of herself she never looked people in the eyes. Her whole persona was that of a beaten and whipped child.

And now suddenly everything had changed.

Tamar awoke to a new world. In this new world she was an attractive girl! She had nice clothes and ate well. As she began to eat better she began to feel better. Instead of being a skinny girl she began to fill out and became even more attractive.

Ha-Melitz kept her family supplied with water so now she could bathe regularly. This made her hair to shine.

No longer did she meekly walk to and from the market place! Now her head was up and her eyes were looking into everyone else's eyes.

But she was not prepared for what she saw.

Years of feeling invisible and unwanted had caused her to crave attention. Her validation was based on what people thought about her. If they were envious of her it made her feel powerful.

There were many eligible bachelors in Dannah. Tamar had been only vaguely aware of them until now.

As she walked to the market she began to notice several of the young men smiling at her. Many of these same young men had made fun of her before, but now they were acting as if they were glad to see her.

She had gone from invisible to being the town celebrity overnight. Where once she doubted that she would even have a bridesmaid at her wedding, now she had too many wanting that honor. It was hard to process for Tamar.

On the one hand it felt very good to know that people liked her now. On the other hand she knew it was only because of who she was marrying that anyone cared. If Jedidiah were to break the engagement for any reason, Tamar would once again go back into obscurity.

She thought about this often. One of the young men was teasing her and asked if she was still going to marry Jedidiah. *"Of course I am!"* she answered, *"Why do you ask?"*

"He may have changed his mind! Sometimes men do that!" he said back to her.

This made Tamar angry, and she let him know it. But truthfully, this thought had crept into her thinking already.

One night as she lay in bed thinking about all of these things, she thought, *"Maybe Jedidiah has changed his mind."*

The more that she dwelled upon that thought the more she began to believe it. After all, it had already been a long wait. How did she know he would keep his word? Maybe he wasn't coming at all. Ha-Melitz might be lying to cover for his friend.

As this thought germinated in her mind she began to think that maybe she should consider alternatives. If Jedidiah didn't love her, maybe someone else would.

There were indeed several young men in Dannah, perhaps one of them would love her? None of them were as handsome as Jedidiah, but they would expect far less out of her than he did.

That next morning Tamar got up early so that she would have time to get ready. She put in extra work to make herself look beautiful this day. She was going to walk closer than usual to Ahaz to see if he would flirt with her. As long as she could remember she liked Ahaz. He was the most handsome man in the village.

As Tamar slowly walked past him she looked him in his eyes.

"Tamar, you look more beautiful than I've ever seen you look before" he said to her. It was clear that he was interested in her.

She knew better than to flirt with him, after all she was a married woman. But the way that he looked at her made her feel good. Ahaz was easy going. She wouldn't have to learn anything to please him.

Tamar's face blushed slightly as Ahaz smiled.

She smiled back at him and asked him how he was doing. They continued in conversation for several minutes before Ha-Melitz walked up to them. When Tamar saw him coming she rolled her eyes and grinned at Ahaz, *"My guardian is here! I guess I have to leave"* she said.

She wanted Ahaz to know that she wasn't happy. She hoped he would take the bait. What she didn't realize is that she wasn't the one fishing, Ahaz was.

For Tamar it seemed so innocent. Yet it was as if a door was opened and something came in and something went out. Tamar began to seek out Ahaz every time she got a chance. They would laugh and talk and flirt.

There was no doubt that Tamar knew she was doing wrong, but this was the first time she had ever felt so good about herself. She reasoned, *"Why shouldn't I feel good about myself for a change?"*

The clothes she wore and the food she ate came from Jedidiah, and she was using his gifts to win Ahaz!

Ha-Melitz was aware of the situation, and he confronted Tamar about it.

"Oh he is just an old friend" she would say. *"There's nothing to it! He's like a brother to me."*

After being confronted by Ha-Melitz, Tamar began to be sneakier when she met Ahaz.

Ahaz knew better too, but he didn't care. He wasn't interested in having a wife. He didn't care about Tamar's happiness. He was only interested in Tamar's money. Everyone in Dannah knew that Jedidiah had given Tamar enough money to live on.

When Tamar came to the market she would hold several silver coins in her hands for all to see. It was her way of showing everyone how wealthy she was now.

Ahaz also hated the little town of Dannah. It offered him no hope and no way out. To escape it he would use Tamar just as he would use a tool or a weapon. They meant nothing to him. They were only a means to an end, and so was she.

He would say anything, and do anything that would get him what he wanted in life. Already he had hurt many people, but he simply did not care.

Ahaz knew that Tamar had money. It may not have been a lot, but it was far more than anyone else in the town had.

If he could convince her that they were really in love perhaps she would run away with him. Once they were together he would take her money and leave her somewhere.

Greed absolutely consumed Ahaz, and he would do anything to satisfy his lusts. It was all that he cared about. People meant nothing to him. Possessions only meant something to him if they made him happy. If they stopped making him happy he got rid of them.

Tamar had heard stories about how Ahaz had brought shame on a young girl in another town. But she chose not to believe them. She believed that this was different. In her mind Ahaz clearly loved her.

Slowly and quietly, Ahaz began to plot what to do. He told Tamar that they would slip away in the dark of the night and go to Egypt. Once there they could do anything that they wanted. There was no limit to what a person could do in Egypt. They would be free to live their lives and be happy together.

Ahaz told Tamar all of the good that he knew about Egypt. What he didn't know he just made up. He knew that there was a lot of evil there, but he didn't tell her that part of the story. After all, he didn't plan on keeping her anyway. He only wanted her money.

Meanwhile Ha-Melitz was concerned about his charge. She had not been acting right for a while, and her attitude was downright rotten!

Two weeks prior Jedidiah had made the trip to Dannah to bring supplies for Tamar. He really came to see her, but she wasn't interested in seeing him. She had been very quiet and withdrawn. One might even say that she had been rude.

It broke Ha-Melitz's heart to watch his friend suffer. Jedidiah was obviously sad when he rode off that night. Ha-Melitz knew that it had to be a long, sad ride back to Jerusalem for Jedidiah.

Tamar had started out so good. For a while it seemed that his work would be easy! But then Ahaz came on the scene. From that point on there had been increasing signs that Tamar was not behaving as a bride should.

On this particular night, Ha-Melitz could not sleep. From His window he could see Tamar's home. All of the lights were out and the family should be asleep, but he felt uneasy.

As he stared at her home he didn't realize that Tamar was already outside waiting for Ahaz. She had slipped out a side window.

She had gathered all of her money and her new clothes that Jedidiah had given her and sneaked out like a thief. For really that is all that she was.

She had entered into a covenant with Jedidiah, and now she was breaking it.

In her mind she could justify everything that she had done until she thought about God. That is when she had to quickly start thinking about something else. God convicted her of what she was doing, for what she was feeling, and for lying to Jedidiah.

It was written in the Law, *"But if you fail to keep your word, then you will have sinned against the LORD, and you may be sure that your sin will find you out."* **Numbers 32:23**

Every time that God spoke to Tamar she would make herself think of being happy with Ahaz in Egypt. A person may change their mind but that will not change God's mind. His Word is eternal and sure. If He spoke a word it is everlasting.

Tamar knew this was true, but she was tired of waiting for Jedidiah. She had come to believe many things that were not true. She could quickly list them in her mind; maybe he didn't really love her? Perhaps she wouldn't be happy with him? Maybe he was really a mean person?

She could reason all sorts of scenarios, but in her heart she knew better. She knew that Jedidiah was every bit as good as he seemed to be. One thing he was not was a hypocrite, and deep down in her heart she knew it.

On a deeper level she realized that she was only pleasing her flesh. But the still, small voice of her conscience was getting quieter all of the time. She kept ignoring it and soon she wouldn't hear it at all.

Tamar heard quiet footsteps coming towards her from behind the house. It was Ahaz. She ran to him and they kissed. This was their first kiss, and Tamar had dreamed about this moment. But something felt wrong when they kissed. It wasn't at all like she thought it would be.

Ahaz wasn't behaving like he was glad to see her either. She thought *"Maybe he is just nervous?"*

In reality Ahaz was nervous, very nervous! He wasn't worried about what happened to Tamar. He never loved her anyway. He was nervous that she wouldn't give him the money. He was nervous that she might figure him out before he could take it from her. Most of all, he was afraid that they might get caught before he could implement his plan.

He hoped to at least get her as far away from Dannah as possible before she realized what he was up to. If he could he would take her all the way to Raphia. But if not he would knock her down and rob her along the way.

He would have to put on a good show if he was going to be able to fool her.

"Tamar my love!" he whispered, *"we must go now if we are to get away!"*

He took her by the hand and led her out of the village to where he had two horses tied up. Helping Tamar up on hers he heard the money rattle in her bag. This might be easier than he thought!

He led her eastward toward the town of Raphia. Raphia was named after the particular type of palm trees that grew in that area. It was situated along the Mediterranean Coast near the Egyptian border.

It would take most of the night to get there. Ahaz had some very unsavory friends who lived in Raphia. Once he reached their house he could dispose of Tamar and be gone.

Initially he thought of taking her money and riding off, leaving Tamar standing by the road. But then he began to think about his friends.

"They might actually want to pay for a young virgin," he thought.

"Maybe my friends will like her?" he thought. He didn't really care one way or another what happened to her. He didn't care if she lived or died.

"What was the difference?" he thought, *"One girl is the same as another."*

Tamar was having misgivings about what they were doing. Her parents and her village would be disappointed of course, but she felt bad for Jedidiah. He had done nothing to warrant this, and yet she was going to hurt him deeply.

All through the night as they rode Tamar tried to shake the feeling that she was in terrible danger. But it lingered and grew stronger.

It was after morning when Tamar and Ahaz reached Raphia. Raphia was a small fishing village and many of the men were already at sea trying to catch fish.

Ahaz had been here several times and he knew where to find his friends. Riding past the market place he led Tamar down a dingy back alley until they came to an ugly and rundown house.

In the house lived Amnon and his sons. They survived mostly by cheating and stealing whatever they could. Ahaz planned on making a deal with them for Tamar. Perhaps they would pay him for her?

Tamar was becoming increasingly nervous. Something was very wrong, but she didn't know what to do. Looking at Ahaz she spoke, *"Are you sure this is safe? It doesn't feel right!"*

"These are old friends of mine, we will be fine" he replied. *"You give me the money and I will take care of everything."*

Although she knew better, she pulled out the money bag and handed it to him.

Smiling broadly he winked at her, *"Just wait here, I will be right back."*

Ahaz was careful to hide the money. He knew the people in the house would kill him if they knew he had it. Knocking on the door he called out, *"Hello, is my friend Salah home? Is Amnon my friend still here? This is your good friend Ahaz!"*

Slowly the door opened just a bit and Ahaz leaned in to whisper something to the person inside of the doorway. Then without looking back at Tamar he went in, leaving her outside not knowing what to do.

Tamar was right to feel nervous here. This family was not to be trusted. The father of the house was a man named Amnon. He had been run out of Judah for stealing, and had a price on his head if he returned.

He lived in Raphia because it was considered Egyptian territory, but it was semi-independent and was ruled by a town council. They didn't care for Amnon's family, and would have evicted them if they could have found a good reason.

But Tamar didn't know any of that. She only knew that she was scared, and felt as if she should flee.

For a few minutes Tamar could hear the muffled sounds of people talking from inside of the house, and then it got quiet. She sat nervously on her horse, wondering if she shouldn't flee. Finally Ahaz stepped out of the doorway followed by a young man named Salah.

Grinning at Tamar, Salah looked back at Ahaz and said, *"Alright, we have a deal!"*

Tamar wondered what was going on. Turning her head back towards the direction she had come from she began to pull on the horse's reins to flee. That was when she felt a strong hand grab her arm. It was Salah. He yanked her off of the horse and threw her to the ground roughly.

"Fifty shekels? I would have asked more!" Salah said to Ahaz. *"But a deal is a deal."*

Tamar looked at Ahaz expecting help, but all that he did was laugh. She now knew that her feelings of dread were well founded. The shock of the realization that Ahaz didn't love her caused Tamar to break out crying.

As the tears streamed down her face, the men only laughed harder. It was clear that she meant absolutely nothing to either of them.

"You belong to Salah now" Ahaz said, *"Have fun!"*

Laughing, he jumped on his horse and grabbed the lead rope on Tamar's horse and rode away. That was the last time that Tamar ever saw him.

Kicking and screaming Tamar was dragged into Amnon's house.

"Shut up or I'll kill you!" shouted Salah. *"You belong to me now. Do you understand? You are my slave!"*

"I don't belong to anybody! Let me go!" Tamar shrieked, but to no avail. Salah was too strong for her.

Waiting inside was his father and his two older brothers. They all came at her at once and held her down.

Then with the help of his father and two brothers, he tied her up, beat her and raped her. As he attacked her Tamar kept screaming for help, but no help came. If any neighbors heard her cries they were afraid to get involved. Horror gave way to shock, and Tamar stopped screaming.

There is probably nothing more inhumane for a person to do than to rape another human being. It is demonic and cruel. It denies a person's humanity and debases them lower than an animal.

Rape cruelly robs a girl of all that is pure in her, and leaves her scarred for life. What is done can never be undone.

Amnon and his family did not care about Tamar. To them she was only valuable if she gave them pleasure. Her needs simply did not exist.

That night Tamar lived through an ordeal that can only be described as hellish. Every bit of dignity she had was taken from her as one after another of Amnon's sons abused her. There was no pity for her tears or her pleading. They acted like mad animals attacking their prey.

The next few months were a continuation of that horror for Tamar. She was being held captive in a strange land by the meanest people she had ever seen. Othniel would have been better to her than they were.

She wasn't a wife to Salah. He treated her worse than he treated his dog. Anytime that he was gone he either tied her up, or left one of his brothers or father to watch her.

His brothers were much older than Salah and every bit as cruel. At first they would fight like savage animals for the right to sleep with her. But after the first few weeks they didn't bother fighting anymore.

Repeatedly she was abused and beaten. If she wept she was beaten. If she spoke when she wasn't supposed to speak she was beaten. Her looks deteriorated rapidly from the abuse. As she lost her looks the family treated her even worse.

All that she wanted was to die.

Even if she was to be set free there was no way for her to go back home. Ahaz may have gone back to Dannah. Maybe he was telling stories about her to her friends and family?

All Tamar could think about was, *"How did I let this happen?"*

There was no place for her to go. All she could think of was dying to get free from her miserable life. Salah made sure that Tamar was never allowed to have a knife or any sharp instruments. He wasn't afraid of her killing herself, but he was afraid that she might use it on one of them.

Tamar had made a mess out of her life. Jedidiah would have been so kind to her. She would never have needed anything if she had just waited on him.

But by now Ha-Melitz would have told him everything that had happened. Jedidiah would have probably found a new wife, and even if he didn't, he would surely never want her back.

When they met she was just a shy virgin girl. Now she was ruined. There was nobody who would help her and she knew it. Death seemed to be the only way out.

One thing that Tamar thought was true; Jedidiah did know that she had run away. But what she couldn't imagine was that he still wanted to marry her.

He had his friends scouring the countryside looking for her. Even in Raphia they looked for her, but there was no way for them to find her in Amnon's house. No one in the town had seen her ride in with Ahaz, so they didn't know she was there.

Several times Jedidiah's friends scoured the streets looking for her, but they never imagined that she was being held as a slave. It never occurred to any of them that Ahaz had sold her.

Jedidiah couldn't have comprehended that Ahaz wouldn't love Tamar. In fact, he assumed that they were happily married by now. He just had to be sure that she was happy, and then he would let her go.

The month's passed and Tamar was once again skinny and dirty. Her hair was a matted mess, and she was hungry most of the time. Amnon's family seemed to eat nothing but fish and onions. Tamar was starving, and so she ate what scraps that they gave her. But she hated the food she was forced to eat.

With each new day she hated herself even more. She hated her life, she hated Amnon and his boys, but most of all she hated Ahaz. All that she imagined her life would be like with Ahaz had been an illusion.

At least in Dannah she had had some measure of self-respect. Now she had nothing. She had been among the poorest in Dannah, but she was known to be kind and pure. In Amnon's house the family dog was treated better than she was.

Late one night after the family had gone to sleep she wept silently with her face to the wall.

"Oh mighty God, I have sinned terribly against you and against my husband. I am not worthy of either of you, but I beg You for mercy tonight. Please, either kill me or set me free!"

As the warm tears flowed down her grimy face Tamar felt hopeless. Why would a holy God pay any attention to her?

She hadn't realized it yet, but God doesn't answer prayers based on merit. He answers prayers based on faith. He demands repentance. It had taken Tamar reaching the very bottom, but she finally had repentance and a little faith. That was more than enough for God to be able to help her.

Chapter seven: Abiel and Jedidiah in Jerusalem

In Jerusalem Abiel was very troubled. His son was in mourning. He wouldn't eat and he barely slept. If this kept up he might lose his son too. Something must be done right away.

He knew that the only way to find Tamar was to find Ahaz, so he sent Ha-Melitz on a special mission.

"Go until you locate Ahaz and then use whatever force is necessary to bring word about Tamar back!" he said. *"If she is pleased to live with Ahaz, then at least we will know it. This is like a funeral where there is no body to bury! Jedidiah must either win her back or let her go."*

Ha-Melitz left immediately for Dannah. He had heard rumors about Ahaz going to Egypt, but no one could say for sure if it was true. He must know. If necessary he would go all of the way to Egypt to find Ahaz and Tamar.

Arriving in Dannah that afternoon Ha-Melitz caused quite a stir. They never expected to see him again. Why would he come now? What could he possibly want? They thought that perhaps he came to imprison Tamar's family. But he didn't go to their house. Instead he went to Ahaz's house.

Knocking on the door he stood patiently waiting. He could hear muffled footsteps inside but no one came to the door. *"Perhaps they are afraid?"* he thought.

"I am not here to cause you any harm I swear!" he cried out. *"But I am on an urgent mission from my master. I only wish to speak to your son Ahaz. I mean him no harm I swear it."*

Slowly the door opened and he could see Ahaz's father staring at him with a frightened look.

"Our son is not home sir. I swear to you we have neither seen nor heard from him since that night that he left" he answered solemnly.

Ha-Melitz already assumed this much, but he needed to know where Ahaz and Tamar had gone.

"I just want to know where they went. I swear to you that neither one of them will be hurt in the least. I only wish to talk to Tamar for a few moments, that's all" he replied.

"Well, we think that he might have taken her to Egypt. He always talked about going there" Ahaz's father answered.

Ha-Melitz thought for a moment about what he should do. If she is in Egypt they may never see her again. He would have to try anyway!

"Then answer me this please, which way would Ahaz have gone to Egypt?" he said.

"More than likely he would have gone along the coastal road. It runs through Raphia. He has a friend there named Salah the son of Amnon. Perhaps they have seen them there? You might try it at least, and please sir, don't hurt my son."

"I am not interested in your son. I only am interested in Tamar!" Ha-Melitz spoke as he turned away from the door.

"Why? Why would you want anything to do with her now?" answered Ahaz's father.

Ha-Melitz didn't bother to answer him. He knew Ahaz's father wouldn't understand anyway. He was going to try to bring Tamar back to face Jedidiah if it killed him.

His love for his friend was all that mattered. Jedidiah loved Tamar, so he would find her for Jedidiah.

Ha-Melitz entered Raphia early in the morning. This was a very unfriendly town. It was full of sailors and fishermen from all around the Mediterranean Sea. The people in Raphia were especially unfriendly to Jews, and they could tell by looking at Ha-Melitz that he was a Jew.

It would not be easy to find Amnon's house. He had to spend several gold coins before he was able to locate someone who would give him the right information.

He finally found an elderly man who knew them and told him where they lived.

"You had better keep your dagger close if you are going to visit those jackals!" the man told him.

"I will, and thank you sir" said Ha-Melitz

Upon arriving at Amnon's house Ha-Melitz thought about the man's warning. He would keep his dagger close, and he would also carry his rod with him, just in case.

Knocking on the door with his rod he was startled to hear someone shouting, *"Go away!"*

Ignoring their command he knocked again, *"I need to talk to Amnon please."*

"Why?" came a coarse reply.

From inside of the house Tamar could hear the conversation.

"That voice!" she thought, *"It sounds like Ha-Melitz!"* Her heart pounded with excitement. *"He might help me!"* she thought.

Peering out of the doorway Amnon looked Ha-Melitz over carefully *"What is it that you want to know?"*

"I am here to inquire about Ahaz of Dannah, and a young girl named Tamar. Tell me, have you seen them? I will pay you for helping me locate the girl." Ha-Melitz answered as firmly as he could.

"Ahaz went off towards Egypt. He sold us the girl. She now belongs to my son Salah" Amnon answered.

"He sold her?" Ha-Melitz couldn't believe it, *"what do you mean he sold her?"*

"What is that any of your concern? Are you her father?" asked Salah as he poked his head out of the doorway.

"I am her guardian. What is the price for Tamar? Tell me and I will gladly give it." Ha-Melitz said.

"I paid fifty pieces of silver for her. But I am not interested in selling her. She is my slave and I enjoy her company. I suggest that you go away while you can. I don't like your attitude." Salah replied.

He could tell that Ha-Melitz was worried about Tamar. Somehow it gave Salah a perverted pleasure to know someone was suffering. He enjoyed making Ha-Melitz unhappy.

Ha-Melitz could see the man and his son both had their hands on their daggers. He would need help to rescue Tamar. But at least he knew where she was. Jedidiah would want to hear what he knew so he backed away. But he kept his hand on his dagger, and his eyes on the men.

"Perhaps we will talk again!" he said as he mounted his horse.

"I suggest that you never bother anyone in this house again if you know what is good for you! Now go!" shouted Amnon as Salah pointed his knife at Ha-Melitz.

Grudgingly Ha-Melitz backed away. It was not in his nature to allow evil to win, even for a day. But he had to get back to Jerusalem as quickly as possible so that he could tell Abiel and Jedidiah.

It took a little over two days for Ha-Melitz to get back to Jerusalem. Abiel was the first to meet him.

"Any news of my daughter?" he asked.

This struck Ha-Melitz as being odd. Why would Abiel still call Tamar his daughter after what she had done to his son?

"Yes my lord, I have found her. But she is being held as a captive slave in Raphia" he said sadly.

This was something that Abiel hadn't considered. *"Tamar is a slave? How did this happen?"* he asked.

"Apparently Ahaz tricked her into going there, and then he sold her as a slave to the lowest type of people in Raphia. I fear for her life in that home" Ha-Melitz said to him.

"We must tell Jedidiah. He will want to leave immediately." Abiel said as he turned to find Jedidiah.

Jedidiah was sitting in the courtyard praying when Abiel and Ha-Melitz walked towards him. It was obvious that he had lost weight, and it was also clear to see that he had been crying.

Hearing their footsteps he raised his head slightly. He knew that his father had sent Ha-Melitz to find out about Tamar's whereabouts.

He had begun to believe that maybe Tamar was happy with Ahaz, and wouldn't want to see him again.

"My lord, I have sad news of Tamar." said Ha-Melitz.

Looking at Ha-Melitz and then his father it was clear that Jedidiah did not understand what he meant. He thought that she was dead.

"How did she die?" he said as tears filled his eyes.

"She lives, but she is in great danger!" Ha-Melitz said to him.

"You mean she is alive? Where is she?" Jedidiah asked. His eyes had looked glassy, but now they sparkled with energy.

"She was sold as a slave to the family in Raphia" Ha-Melitz said. *"Ahaz the scoundrel sold her for fifty pieces of silver!"*

"Didn't you offer to buy her back from them?" Jedidiah asked.

"Yes of course, but they refused to sell her. I fear for her life" Ha-Melitz answered. His concern for Tamar was real. He felt uneasy leaving Raphia without her, but he had no choice at the time.

Jedidiah practically shouted, *"Let us go at once and save her!"* as he leapt to his feet.

Jedidiah had not shown any vitality for weeks, but suddenly he seemed to come alive. Leaping to his feet he ran into the house to get his weapons, and more than enough money.

"We will try to reason with them, and if that fails we will force them to set her free!" he said as he sprinted into the house.

Ha-Melitz thought it would be better for Jedidiah to let him and some servants go rescue Tamar.

"Let me and some of your best servants go rescue her, my friend. You should stay here." He said, but Jedidiah ignored him.

Turning back to where Abiel had been standing Ha-Melitz hoped that he at least would listen to reason. But Abiel had taken off the other way towards the servant's quarters.

"If it is necessary to fight you will not fight alone" he said as he left them to gather his servants. It was obvious that neither the father nor the son were willing to wait for him to save Tamar.

Pulling Jedidiah aside, Ha-Melitz asked him quietly, *"Are you able to ride so soon my friend?"*

"Able? Yes, I am able, and anxious!" was his reply.

Initially, when Jedidiah found out that Tamar had ran away he was in shock. He neither ate nor slept. But finally shock gave way to grief. For weeks he had mourned as if she had died.

Most people assumed that Jedidiah would move on from Tamar. *"He could have done better than her"* they reasoned.

But they did not understand how he loved her. He knew that Tamar didn't love him the way that he loved her; but he also knew that she didn't know what true love was.

For her, love meant receiving things. For Jedidiah, love was about giving. This was something that Tamar never learned at home. It was all foreign to her. He wanted to at least have the chance to show her what true love was like. Maybe Tamar would never understand, but he knew that at least he must try.

As they prepared to leave, Ha-Melitz began to think about the potential for danger in Raphia. If it came down to having to fight Salah and his family he was worried that Jedidiah might get hurt. The people in that town would probably back one of their own against Jews, even if it was Amnon.

"Perhaps I should take your father's servants and go after the girl while you wait here?" he said again to Jedidiah.

"No", Jedidiah answered, *"I must go. I am her legal husband, and only I have the legal right to take her"*

Jedidiah was correct; only a legally married husband had any lawful claim to Tamar now. Even her own father couldn't have rescued her. And even Jedidiah may not be able to help her.

Although he knew Jedidiah well, Ha-Melitz couldn't quite understand why he still wanted Tamar. *"Jedidiah my friend, why do you insist on helping to free a girl who cared so little about you?"* he asked as they loaded their horses.

Looking into Ha-Melitz's eyes for a moment he slowly answered, *"Because I love her!"*

Ha-Melitz pressed him further, *"Isn't it possible that she will never love you in the way that you love her? She might even leave you again."*

Jedidiah sighed deeply, *"Yes, it is possible. It may be that she will never understand me or love me. But I cannot decide this based solely on what she might do. I have made my choice because I love her.*

Let me tell you why I feel this way. Once, long ago my mother was a poor girl in a small village up north. My father ran into her, I mean he literally ran into her, and knocked her down!

As he helped her to her feet he looked into her eyes, and it was love at first sight. She had been born as a slave to a wealthy merchant from Sidon.

My father sold everything that he possessed to buy her freedom. So great was his love for her that he even sold his shoes. He had just enough to free her.

And then, my father gave my mother two choices; first she had the freedom to leave him and go where she wished.

Or secondly, she could marry him. She married him and God blessed them mightily. I suppose there is a lot of my father in me. I will set Tamar free and give her the same choice that my father gave my mother. You must understand that I too fell in love at first sight.

<u>There is no greater love than this</u>. *I would gladly die for her, even if she never loves me back."*

Ha-Melitz looked his friend in the eyes again, *"I believe I understand. But I feel that this will not be an easy thing. I have feelings of dread for some reason. We had best be very careful."*

"I agree. I too have misgivings about this; but Ha-Melitz my friend, love compels me to go. To sit at home while she is imprisoned would surely kill me. I must do whatever is necessary to free her. If she rejects me then, at least I will know that I did what I could.

If we love someone, I mean really love someone, how can we sit by and let them suffer?"

Ha-Melitz nodded his head in approval; he knew that Jedidiah meant every word that he spoke.

Just then Abiel walked up to them. He had brought his horse for Jedidiah to ride. No one was allowed to sit on Abiel's prize stallion. Not even Jedidiah had ridden it. Ha-Melitz realized how much that both father and son wanted to rescue Tamar.

If Tamar had been living happily in Egypt they would have left her alone. But now that they knew that she was being held captive it seemed to invigorate both of them.

Speaking softly to his son, Abiel said, *"My son, I know what you feel for Tamar. You and I are just alike. I felt the same way about your mother. Do what love tells you to do, and may God be with you, and make you able to bring my daughter home again."*

"I will save her father, God willing." Jedidiah replied.

Mounting their horses they began the journey to Raphia. Abiel had made certain to send his strongest servants to help them. They were loyal and well able to fight if necessary.

It would take them about two full days to reach Raphia. If they pushed it they could make it in a day and half. That would put them in Raphia about noon on the second day.

Jedidiah told them to prepare for a long ride; it was obvious he intended to get there as fast as possible.

Back in Amnon's house Tamar was unsure of what to do. Ha-Melitz had offered to buy her freedom, could that mean that Jedidiah still loved her? But how could he love her after what she had done?

"Perhaps he wishes to imprison me in Jerusalem?" she thought. *"If he does I will not complain about it. He at least will be kind in judgment. It would still be better than being here."*

One thing she knew, she had to get free somehow.

Salah had thought about Ha-Melitz's offer. He was growing tired of Tamar anyway. He and his father were willing to do almost anything for a few coins. Perhaps they should have sold her?

Amnon was puzzled by the whole thing. Who were these people that wanted a dirty slave girl?

The next evening Salah asked Tamar about Ha-Melitz.

Grabbing her by her hair he pulled her head back and asked her, *"Who was that man? Why was he looking for you?"*

"He is the friend of Jedidiah of Jerusalem" she answered.

"So you have rich friends do you? I have heard of this man Jedidiah, and his father Abiel. They are very influential people. You told me that you were from a poor family in Dannah! Why is this person looking for you?" he asked angrily.

Tamar began to tell her story to Salah. Weeping she recounted how she had betrayed Jedidiah because she thought Ahaz loved her.

Seeing her weep did not cause Salah to show compassion. In fact, it made him angry.

"Shut that up!" he said as he slapped her in the face. *"Anyone stupid enough to think Ahaz loved them deserves what they get!"* he laughed.

Although Tamar knew she wasn't supposed to cry she couldn't help herself. *"He lied to me, he promised me happiness, and now I am a slave!"*

Slapping her again Salah was growing visibly angrier, *"Shut that up or I will kill you right now!"*

Drawing back his hand he hit her even harder. Tamar screamed in pain as he hit her in the mouth. This only made Salah become more violent. Now instead of slapping her he was using his fists.

"You worthless piece of garbage! Shut up, shut up, shut up!" he screamed as he pulled her hair with one hand and punched her with the other.

Some men like to feel powerful by harming someone who can't fight back. Salah was like this. He enjoyed hurting people who were unable to retaliate.

Tamar ducked her head to escape the punches he was throwing when she spied his dagger on his belt. Grabbing it she pulled it from its sheath and stabbed Salah in his stomach.

Now it was Salah's turn to scream and cry.

"Father, help me! That slave girl stabbed me!" he screamed as he staggered back.

Tamar stood holding the knife when Amnon came into the room. Without speaking a word he hit Tamar with his fist, knocking her unconscious.

When Tamar awoke she realized that she was outside. The evening sun was setting on the sea in what would have been a beautiful picture; if she was somewhere else besides Raphia.

The village elders were discussing what to do about her. They all knew the family of Amnon, and none of them felt the least bit sorry for Salah. They would have been happy to see Amnon and his sons leave Raphia. Besides, Salah would live, so Tamar shouldn't be put to death.

They actually felt sorry for Tamar. But she was a slave, and slaves were forbidden by law from fighting back, no matter how evil their masters might be.

There were many abused slaves in Raphia, and they were all anxiously watching to see what happened to Tamar.

The oldest member of the council spoke, *"At the very least we must tie her to the post and flog her with a whip"* he said. *"If we don't do at least that more slaves might think to do what she has done. We cannot allow them to believe that they have any right to defend themselves."*

They all agreed, *"Tomorrow let her be punished before everyone in edge of town at the whipping post. That way every slave will be able to see what happens when they fight back, and they will fear."*

The whip was made of straps with sharp pieces of metal, stone, thorns and glass tied to each strip. A prisoner could be beaten with it thirty-nine times.

Most people went into shock from the pain and loss of blood. In her state Tamar would most likely die and she knew it.

"Why God? Why did this happen? I never meant to end up here! Please help me! Please God! Don't let me be beaten by the whip" she begged God.

No one took pity on her. She was a slave, and slaves had no rights in their view.

Tamar was tied up next to the guard house that the soldiers used. It was a stone building with a hard, cold floor.

She couldn't sleep because the pain and the fear kept her awake. Amnon had beaten her even after knocking her out. He was a very cruel man like his son. He got a perverse pleasure in causing pain in other people.

The next morning brought Tamar no relief. By this time one eye had swollen almost completely shut. Her lips were protruding in a grotesque manner from being punched so severely. Her body ached as a result of the beatings. She was slightly disoriented from dehydration. No one had bothered to give her either food or water. They watered their dogs but not Tamar.

The guards simply walked over and around her like she was a pile of garbage. To them she was not even a human being.

The sun was nearing midday before anyone spoke to her, and even then it wasn't out of kindness, but anger.

"Come on slave!" yelled one of the soldiers as he grabbed her hands.

Untying one end of the rope from the wall, he led her to the edge of town.

She was so weak and frightened that she was almost unable to walk. *"Please have mercy on me!" she* begged him as he pulled her along. But it was no use; he had no mercy to give.

"Oh come on now. I am not going to carry you! If you make me I will drag you there!" he shouted.

Stumbling along Tamar was pleading with God to let her die quickly. She had nothing to offer God as a bargain, and she knew that God didn't make bargains anyway. She only was asking for mercy.

"I deserve everything I have gotten Lord. I only beg of you to let me die quickly so that my suffering might come to an end. Please show me mercy, not justice!"

Mercy by its very nature is undeserved kindness. That is what Tamar was asking for and surprisingly it is what she would receive.

As they reached the edge of the village, the people began to shout obscenities at her.

"Why are they happy to see me suffer?" she thought. *"They don't even know me or what I have been through! Couldn't one of them have pity on me?"*

But this was a cruel town filled with hatred. They enjoyed watching another human being suffer. To them, Tamar's torture was just sport. They would cheer the whipping, and then go on with their lives as if nothing had happened.

Tamar looks at the whip

The guard jerked her upright and tied her to the post. That way she would have to stand the whole time. She would be an easy target for the man using the whip.

Suddenly she heard two familiar voices shouting at her. It was Amnon and Salah. Knowing that they were going to get to watch her being whipped only made her sadder.

"Oh God, please just let me die quickly!" she cried.

Tamar takes a deep breath as she waits to be punished

Weeping, Tamar hung her head and prepared for the inevitable. She was sure that there was no one in the city of Raphia who cared for her.

Chapter eight: My Redeemer lives!

In the midst of the uproar a small group of strangers appeared. They were unnoticed at first; most people were focused on the spectacle of Tamar being punished. Jedidiah walked through the crowd and to the soldier who was starting to draw back the whip.

"Stay your hand for a moment please" he said.

"Why should I? Who are you?" the soldier asked angrily.

"I am Jedidiah, son of Abiel of Jerusalem and this is Tamar, she is my lawful wife who was stolen from me" spoke Jedidiah. His voice sounded calm and strong as he spoke, and the whole crowd grew silent as they waited to see what would happen next.

Stepping forward from the crowd and still holding his side where he had been stabbed, Salah shouted at him, *"Tamar belongs to me! Ahaz sold her to me for fifty shekels! She was his property of her own free will. She left her father's home with Ahaz, and he sold her so now I am her master!"*

"Fifty shekels?" asked Jedidiah incredulously. How could someone think Tamar was worth so little? *"I will gladly pay more than that for her. Set your price."*

Salah realized that Tamar would probably be dead after being flogged with the whip. He didn't want her back anyway because he didn't trust her. He might as well sell her for as much as he could get.

"I want one thousand shekels for her." He said.

"Sold" said Jedidiah without a moment's hesitation. He would pay any price to get her back. *"Return my wife to me now!"*

"Not quite so fast or easy I'm afraid" said the soldier. *"Maybe you don't know why she is here today. She is a slave, and she attacked her master with a dagger. She must be punished for her crime."*

"He bought her under false pretenses; she ought to be set free" said Jedidiah.

"That all may be true where you came from. But in Raphia the law is clear, and she belonged to Salah son of Amnon. He paid a fair price for her and she was legally his slave. Then she stabbed him. The girl must pay the penalty of the law. She is guilty. Nobody doubts the facts of the case!"

Staring at Tamar's bloodied and bruised face, Jedidiah couldn't allow her to suffer anymore.

"I will take her place. That way all can witness justice being served, and the crime will not go unpunished" he said.

Looking up towards Jedidiah, Tamar could see that he had been suffering too. He had dark circles around his eyes and his cheeks were hollow looking. She hadn't realized how much she had hurt him.

"No please don't" she cried, *"Let me pay the price! You are innocent. You haven't done anything wrong, I have. I demand to be the one to pay. Just let me die please, I deserve it!"*

"No, you can't bear the whip in your condition, it would kill you. And I couldn't bear to watch you being whipped. I can stand being whipped, but I cannot take letting you die" he answered her.

Making his way to the post, Jedidiah said, *"Take me in her stead. I am her legal husband; I alone can take her place."*

Tamar's heart was breaking now. *"How could I cause so much evil to one so kind? How could I hurt him so badly! What was I thinking to choose Ahaz over him? And now he wants to take my place? No! He mustn't suffer any more for me. I am not worth it!"*

"No my lord Jedidiah, I am not worth saving. Please just let me die" she pleaded one more time.

"I have decided already my love. My life for yours" he said. And then he looked at the soldier and held out his hands, *"Do your duty sir."*

The soldier looked at his commanding officer as if to ask what he should do.

"Go ahead then" said the commander. *"Give the fool what he wants."*

Salah began to laugh out loud. He found great pleasure in the thought that this rich Jew was going to suffer, and maybe die.

Untying Tamar, two soldiers drug her past Jedidiah to Ha-Melitz. For a brief moment they were able to look in each other's eyes again. Tamar could only see out of one eye due to being beaten so badly. Yet she stared intently at Jedidiah's eyes pleadingly, *"Please don't do this! Please!"* she cried out.

But there was no talking him out of it. When Jedidiah looked at Tamar's bruised and battered face his heart broke. Tears were pouring from his eyes as the soldiers grabbed his hands.

"Are you still sure that you want to take her place?" they asked.

"Of course I am!" he said firmly.

Then they took Jedidiah's hands and tied him to the ring on the post so that he would be an easy target. They then ripped his clothes off of him to shame him. For several minutes the people laughed at him and mocked him. Several spit on him as he waited for the whip.

Then the man with the whip held it up as a sign for the crowd to quiet down. As they joyfully watched, he drew it back slowly and carefully.

Then he swung with all of his might at Jedidiah. It hit with a thud as the ends of the whip dug into his body. The whip spread out as it was swung at Jedidiah. Some of the ends hit him on his head while others hit his back and sides. Wherever the ends hit they cut into his flesh.

Tamar screamed as she watched Jedidiah being beaten. Over and over again the soldier hit him! Blood sprayed the crowd as the whip was ripped back from his body, and they loved it! This was a grand spectacle for them.

When the soldier hit Jedidiah for the thirty-ninth time he laid his whip down. The crowd had been cheering wildly the whole time. They were well aware that Jedidiah was a Jew, and they hated all of the Jews. They began to boo and hiss when the soldier stopped.

Jedidiah had not cried out in pain or tried to get away. It was clear that he meant to take every drop of punishment that they could dish out.

The soldier enjoyed his work that day. Normally there is not much of a crowd when he whipped a prisoner. This day most of the village was cheering him on. And what a prisoner! A rich fool from the city of Jerusalem! What a story he would have to tell his family.

When the beating was over they cut the ropes and let Jedidiah fall to the ground. Ha-Melitz and the servants rushed forward to catch him.

He was a bloody pulp. Many stripes and countless wounds covered his body. He never moved or moaned. He looked as if he was dead.

Tamar fainted.

Walking up to Ha-Melitz, Salah held out his hand. *"Where are my thousand shekels?"* he asked. It was obvious he cared nothing for Tamar.

Without speaking a word to him, Ha-Melitz handed him the money. Then he turned back to his friend. Jedidiah was not moving, and it was difficult to tell if he was even alive. He was swollen and bloody from his head to his feet. The soldier with the whip knew his business for he had been able to inflict the maximum amount of punishment on him. It would take a miracle for Jedidiah to live.

Binding up his body they made a cot to pull behind their horses and they started back to Jerusalem. Normally they could make it in two days, but because Tamar and Jedidiah were both so badly hurt it would take three. Ha-Melitz knew that Jedidiah would probably never survive the trip.

"We will go to the healing house at Succoth. It is closer. One of you will ride to tell his father Abiel the news. We will wait for him there" he said to the servants.

Tamar had been beaten so severely by Amnon and Salah that she couldn't walk. So she rode on the cot with Jedidiah. She tried to tend to him but he remained unconscious.

Tamar couldn't stop crying. Her lips were so badly swollen that it hurt to even talk. Yet she couldn't help but kiss Jedidiah over and over.

She realized that she had never loved him, not really loved him, until now.

That night as they rested Tamar began to question Ha-Melitz about why they had searched for her.

Ha-Melitz answered her, *"We were searching for you because your husband still loves you."*

This made no sense to Tamar. shaking her head she asked him, *"But why? Why would he still love me? It doesn't make sense."*

Ha-Melitz knew that she couldn't begin to understand love. From her childhood she had been taught that love was carnal and fleshly. Her way of understanding love was to believe that love was only an emotion, nothing more.

But true love is far more than an emotion. True love is more important than life itself to the one who possesses it. Nothing is more powerful than love. It is the only way to describe Almighty God- God is love.

Tamar knew none of these things. It was totally foreign to her way of thinking and Ha-Melitz understood this. He knew it would take a long time for her to comprehend how much Jedidiah loved her.

Ha-Melitz had asked Jedidiah the same questions on the journey from Jerusalem to Raphia. Jedidiah had quoted a passage from the Song of Solomon to explain how deeply his love went;

"Much water may not put out love, or the deep waters overcome it: if a man would give all the substance of his house for love, it would be judged a price not great enough." **Song of Solomon 8:7**

He continued, *"That is how my father loved my mother. That is how I feel about Tamar. I can't walk away from my heart you know. It will trouble me until I die if I don't try to save her.*

"Love burns in your heart like the hottest fire. Solomon was right. Nothing can put out the fire once it is lit. True love is worth more than all of the wealth of the earth.

I have fallen deeply and maddeningly in love with Tamar. Either I win her back or die, but I cannot continue without her!" Jedidiah had told him.

Ha-Melitz knew it was true and unless they were able to rescue Tamar, Jedidiah would indeed die out of sorrow.

"Why did Jedidiah come for me? I am not worth saving" Tamar said. *"Why would he suffer for me? I don't understand. I am less than nothing!"*

Ha-Melitz felt pity for Tamar because she never chose to be raised the way that she had been raised.

Looking at her swollen and beaten face he said,

"You don't understand love. You see, you were never valuable because of what you were. You were valuable because of who he is. He loves you, and that has nothing to do with what you have done. It only matters that he has chosen to love you."

It was all too difficult for Tamar to understand.

Shaking her head she spoke slowly, as if to herself, *"How? How could someone so pure and kind love me after what I have done to him? He should hate me! If he had whipped me himself he would have been right in doing it."*

Looking towards Ha-Melitz and then at Jedidiah she said, *"I have sinned against him and his father, and you"* as she started crying again. *"I will never be able to repay him"* said Tamar.

"Love says that you will never have to" answered Ha-Melitz. *"I have known Jedidiah all of my life. When he loves someone, he loves them forever. He told me that he doesn't believe that you ever realized what true love was.*

He said that he wanted to show you. I suppose that if you don't understand love by now, you never will."

Tamar looked at him as if she suddenly realized a great truth, *"I guess you are right; I really have never understood true love. Maybe if he will allow me to I will be able to love him like he has loved me. Do you think there is a chance?"* she asked.

"There will always be a chance, if he lives. As long as he lives he will love you, this I know" Ha-Melitz said. The words now stuck in his throat, *"if he lives!"* it was hard for him to admit it, but his friend might not live.

Tamar shook when he said those words as if a sudden chill had swept her body. *"He must live! God cannot let the Ahaz's and Salah's of the world live, and allow someone as perfect as Jedidiah to die."*

He answered her, *"I am certain that he will live because now he has you back. Your love will give him the strength that he needs."*

Tamar was beginning to understand something of true love; love is giving, not receiving. She would gladly give her life for Jedidiah's. Dying would be far easier than living. But to truly pay him back, she needed to live for him. That would be more difficult to do. But he was worth any amount of suffering and shame.

"I want to repay his sacrifice somehow. I was once a slave and he set me free. I will be his slave forever if he wants me to. If he chooses to imprison me I will not complain. If he wishes to never see me again I will understand. I belong to him without reservation. I will never forgive myself for harming him" she said loudly for all to hear.

Ha-Melitz thought about the things Jedidiah had told him on the journey, *"Maybe she can be saved"* he thought *"I think I see a change in her after all!"*

"You have much to learn about love Tamar" said Ha-Melitz. *"I guess you have never seen true love before. Jedidiah and his father love you. You don't deserve it, that is true, but deserve has nothing to do with love."*

What was the other verse that Jedidiah had quoted to him? Oh yes, it was from the **Song of Solomon 8:6**;

Set me as a seal upon thine heart, as a seal upon thine arm: for love is strong as death.

"Yes" he thought, *"Love is as strong as death."*

The next morning Ha-Melitz was up early preparing for the day ahead when Tamar approached him.

"I fear seeing Abiel again" she said.

"Why?" he asked.

Burying her face in her hands she cried, *"Because, it is my fault that his son was nearly beaten to death. How can I look at him after causing Jedidiah to suffer so much?"*

"Remember this and you will not fear; Jedidiah learned to love from his father. If you have seen the son's love, you have seen the father's love." Ha-Melitz answered her.

In Jerusalem, Abiel had been fasting and praying. He knew about Raphia and the type of people who lived there. It was not the kind of place to visit. A person was much better off passing it by.

If Jedidiah had to fight to get Tamar back he might be hurt. The thought of his son suffering caused him to feel weak. He loved his son with all of his heart, and couldn't bear the thought of losing him.

If he had known the price that Jedidiah had paid to recover Tamar he would have felt much worse.

Two scenarios played out in his mind. One, Tamar and Jedidiah would be reconciled and be married. This was his prayer.

But she might not love his son. If that was true she would be free to do whatever she wished. She might even choose to go back to her family. If she didn't love Jedidiah he would have to learn to go on with his life, no matter how much it hurt to do so.

After the fourth day came and went, Abiel became even more nervous.

He thought to himself, *"it took two days to reach Raphia. If all went well they should have been back today. What is delaying them?"*

That night he couldn't sleep. Those were six of his strongest servants accompanying Jedidiah and Ha-Melitz on the trip. Surely they could protect him?

He wondered if he should have asked his friends for more help.

Meanwhile several miles southwest of Jerusalem, Tamar was making Jedidiah drink water from her hand. He didn't drink much, but he did at least drink a little.

He had a fever now and his swelling was noticeably worse. She knew that he might not survive.

For once in her life she wasn't thinking of herself.

Abiel, meanwhile, was growing increasingly apprehensive. *"Where are they?"* he kept repeating out loud. *"They should have been here by now! I just pray that they are safe."*

It was nearly noon when Abiel heard a rider galloping towards his home at a high rate of speed. Looking out he recognized one of his servants.

"Is all well?" he asked him anxiously.

"My lord Jedidiah is gravely wounded, and the girl Tamar is too. Ha-Melitz took them to Succoth to the healing house. He asked that I should come tell you to come as fast as you can" answered the servant.

Abiel became momentarily weak at the thought of his son being hurt. He had felt in his heart that this would be a dangerous undertaking. He would have gone himself if he could have. He knew that at his age he would have been more of a handicap than a help.

When they first left he had felt a feeling of fear grip him, and he had not been able to shake it. The only comfort that he had was the fact that Ha-Melitz was with Jedidiah. Abiel had complete faith and confidence in him. He knew that Ha-Melitz would defend Jedidiah with his life if necessary.

Ha-Melitz was originally from Succoth, and was very familiar with the place. Abiel knew that if he thought it was necessary to take Jedidiah there instead of bringing him home he should trust him.

He stepped out of the doorway and walked over to the servant, *"What happened? Tell me everything"* he demanded of the servant.

The servant told him everything, from Tamar being tricked by Ahaz to her fighting back against Salah, and how Jedidiah took her place at the whipping post.

"My lord, your son had not regained consciousness at the time I rode on. Ha-Melitz told me to tell you that you must hurry" the servant said in a somber tone.

"You stay here and rest. I will go alone to see my son" Abiel said as he ran towards the stable. It would take him most of the day to reach Succoth, so he must hurry.

The journey to Succoth seemed to be the longest journey of Abiel's life. The sun was setting as he rode into town. Standing at the gate were his servants. Ha-Melitz had told them to wait there until he arrived, and then to bring him to Jedidiah.

As he entered the house he could see from Ha-Melitz's face that Jedidiah was gravely wounded. But he wasn't prepared for what he saw.

Abiel's face became pale, and he almost passed out when he looked at his son. For a minute he felt weak, but he was able to steady himself. His son needed him, so he would have to be strong for his sake.

He didn't initially notice Tamar. She had stepped out of the way when she saw him approaching. If she had been able to she would have ran away. But she couldn't leave Jedidiah.

Abiel leaned over his son and looked at his battered and torn body and began to weep. Jedidiah would carry those scars for the rest of his life.

After several moments he noticed movement in the corner of the room. Abiel turned to see who it was, and that was when he realized it was Tamar.

She was leaning against the wall with her face looking towards the floor. It seemed to Abiel that she was trying to be invisible. He knew that she needed his love and affirmation more than ever.

"Is that you, my daughter Tamar?" he asked.

Tamar's emotions overcame her when she heard Abiel call her his daughter. Dropping to her knees she began to cry uncontrollably.

"I am not worthy to be your daughter my lord!" she said.

Walking to her he lifted her up, and put his arm around her. Then he bent down and kissed her matted hair gently. *"I did not ask you if you were worthy did I? I chose you, remember? I am the one who sought you and found you. You didn't choose me. It will all be alright. You will see"* he assured her.

As Tamar clung to Abiel and cried she heard a weak voice calling her name. It was Jedidiah!

"Tamar? Tamar, Are you alright my love?" he asked.

She was so happy that she couldn't find her voice. Stumbling towards him she half believed that it was only a dream.

Finally finding her voice she said, *"Yes, I am alright now my lord! Now that you live. I couldn't face life if you weren't in it."*

Upon hearing her reply Jedidiah began to weep, but it was tears of joy that he shed. Even at the whipping post he wasn't sure that Tamar wanted him. He realized that his once handsome features were now gone. His face and body were wrecked and ruined.

In his mind he knew that her sin was on his body. It was painful to think that this pain was the result of another's sin. But he would do it all over again if necessary to save her, because he loved her so much.

When he heard Tamar say that she couldn't go through life without him, Jedidiah felt joy in his soul. *"Praise God! She loves me!"* he thought.

Smiling against the pain she felt, Tamar felt strength come back into her. *"He is going to live!"* she thought. If he lived then she knew she must live for him.

It would be several days before Jedidiah could walk again. The soldier had flogged his legs and back so severely that it had torn his muscles. Breathing was painful and difficult for him, and the loss of blood had made him very weak.

Tamar also needed time to heal. Her cheekbones were fractured from the beatings that she had taken. Her lips remained sore, although the swelling was almost gone.

As she walked in the garden behind the healing home she thought how she had never felt more at peace. Her suffering had changed her in every way. She no longer thought of herself first. She finally realized what it meant to truly love someone.

She was so absorbed in her thoughts that she never heard Abiel as he walked out to her. She was somewhat startled by his sudden appearance.

Tamar couldn't have been treated any more kindly than Abiel had treated her, but she couldn't make herself look him in the eyes. She had caused him so much pain that all she felt was guilt when she looked his way.

Instinctively she looked down when she realized who it was. Abiel reached out his hand and lifted Tamar's chin, forcing her to look him in the eyes.

"My daughter, why do you look away when I approach you?" he asked.

"Because, I am so ashamed for what I have done to you, and to Jedidiah. I have caused you so much suffering, and poor Jedidiah may never be the same again. Plus he will carry those awful scars the rest of his life, and it is all my fault" she said as tears rolled off of her cheeks.

"I want you to understand something my child; no one here hates you or blames you. You believed an illusion, and that is all that sin has to offer, an illusion. But sin has a price that must be paid. Jedidiah paid your price for you. It is fully paid so there is no reason to keep on trying to pay it back." Abiel said gently.

"Forever when you look at my son, you will see the proofs of his love for you! I believe that you can be the wife that he deserves."

"How can I live with myself after all that I have done?" she cried.

"I ask you for love's sake to love my son. I believe you can do that now. Don't you?" Abiel's voice was strong and forceful.

Tamar felt strengthened by the thought, *"Yes, I can serve him for love's sake, and not for guilt's sake!"* she said.

Smiling at her, Abiel stared into her blood-shot eyes for a moment, and then he said, *"If you were to serve for guilt's sake, you would eventually grow frustrated trying to repay your debt. Love never grows old. Love him and you will be refreshed."*

"But everyone surely hates me! Every time that they look at Jedidiah's scars they will see me! How can I live in his world? He is so well known, and loved in Jerusalem that they will surely hate me!" it was clear that Tamar was fearful of facing people.

"My child, people fail each other. Even the best make mistakes. Most wounds are hidden in the heart, but nearly everyone has some wounds. Jedidiah was wounded in his heart, but now his heart is healed.

However he now carries on his body the wounds that had been in his heart. I want you to think about that, because the wound you see was already there. Now it is visible, but it is less painful to him because now he has hope.

His heart longs to be with you. You are his reason for living" he said to her.

"I hope that you understand this; he sees no future unless you are in it. Those scars that he will bear on his body should always remind you that they were first in his heart.

"Everything that is hidden must come to light. I know that my son is now better off than he was sitting and longing for you. Can you live with the knowledge that he loves you this much?" he asked her as he looked firmly into her eyes.

"Yes, I understand. I guess I am still worrying about what people think. I have always been bound by that. But now I realize that as long as I have Jedidiah, nothing else matters" she answered him.

Abiel held her close to his bosom as they both shed tears of joy.

"Jedidiah will be whole again. His wounds will heal. The two of you will have a long life together, and I am sure that you will grow closer as the years go by. One day you will have children, then grandchildren. They will undoubtedly ask you about the scars Jedidiah will carry. Don't act embarrassed or ashamed when they ask; tell them the story of Jedidiah's love for you. You see, they too will need to know what true love is" Abiel told her.

"If they know what true love is, they will not fall for the fake" Tamar reasoned out loud.

"Exactly! Rather than being ashamed about yourself, you should be willing to tell everyone about what Jedidiah did! Can't you see?

His sacrifice will set the standard higher. People need a reason to hope and to believe. If a man can love that way, just think how much God loves!"

Abiel was almost shouting now, the thought that God loved us even more than Jedidiah loved Tamar excited him.

"God? Do you think God loves me after what I have done? How is that even possible?" she asked.

In reality, Tamar had avoided even thinking about God. She couldn't bring herself to face Him either. The hurt of failing God and Jedidiah was too much for her to bear.

Abiel answered her, *"Do you fear God? He is greater than Jedidiah isn't He? Of course He loves you! He loves you more than Jedidiah does"*

Tamar looked down at the ground and took a deep breath, *"I prayed that God would let me die when I was in Amnon's house. I would gladly have died at the whipping post that day. But I guess I have not reconciled with God yet. The thought of facing you filled me with such fear, and the thought of facing God does also"* she softly spoke.

"I guess in all of my life I have never actually talked to God unless I was either asking for something, or telling Him what I wanted Him to do. I really don't know how to pray to God" Tamar said, half to herself.

"My child" Abiel said in a kind voice, *"talk to God in the same voice and with the same words that you use when you talk to me. If you have to change your voice to talk to God, you are only talking at Him!"*

Then he said to her, *"Why don't you stay here in the garden until the evening meal is prepared. You can spend your time talking to God. And remember, He knows everything about you and He still loves you!"*

Tamar smiled at his words. He was clearly intent on making her become a believer. *"I will, I promise"* she told him as he walked away.

Chapter nine: A tough choice to make

It took almost two weeks before Jedidiah was healthy enough to return home to Jerusalem. Tamar thought that she would simply go home with him, but Abiel had other plans. One morning as she was once again walking in the garden he went to where she was.

He was smiling at her as he came. *"Do you feel better my daughter?"* he asked.

"Yes, I am almost whole now" she answered confidently.

Abiel said, *"I have been speaking to Jedidiah and Ha-Melitz about everything that has happened. I believe that the devil has tried to destroy you, don't you?"*

"Oh yes, I know he did. I will carry my wounds and my shame forever" she answered.

"Yes, that is the awful secret that the devil never tells the people that he tempts; every sin that we do affects the people we love. And it affects those who love us too. There is a very steep price that must be paid for sin. It is easy to get into sin, but very painful to get out" Abiel replied.

Tamar knew she couldn't explain to Abiel why she had done what she did. What would be the use in trying to justify it? She might as well own up to it, and admit it was her fault.

Looking Abiel in the face she said, *"I can never repay your kindness. I don't even know how to begin. If you threw me into prison I wouldn't complain. I deserve to die. If it weren't for Jedidiah I would prefer to die. But the way that he loves me makes me think that somehow I have to repay him. Even if it is being his slave I am willing."*

Abiel studied Tamar's face for a few moments. He remembered the way that she had looked at Jedidiah when they first met in her father's house. Her suffering had changed her. There was a deep love in her eyes now, but there was also a deep sorrow.

Putting his hand on her shoulder he spoke slowly;

"My wife and I were so in love that we couldn't have lived without each other. I have always prayed that my son would know what that kind of love was like. My prayer has been answered. It hasn't come in the way I would have desired, but I know that he loves you unconditionally. If you will repay him, love him the same way.

Don't ever allow anyone or anything to come between you and Jedidiah. No one can love you like he loves you!"

Tamar was beginning to cry again, *"I swear that I will love him, and only him, until the day that I die!"*

Taking a deep breath, Abiel said, *"I believe you. Now my daughter, we must talk about something. This is going to be very difficult for you, but I must ask you to do this for me; I want you to return to your father's house."*

Tamar felt her heart racing in her chest. She never wanted to go back to Dannah. She couldn't bear the thought of seeing those people again.

"I will do whatever you ask of me" she said, *"but why do I have to go back there?"* she was having trouble breathing now. It seemed that her heart was going to beat out of her chest. In some ways this was as fearful as the whipping post had been in Raphia.

Abiel knew exactly what he was asking of her. It wasn't to punish her for her sins that he wanted her to go. In fact, it was because he loved her so much that he was asking. Carefully he spoke;

"I realize that this is going to be very difficult for you and that you are afraid. I have prayed about this very much, and I believe that you will show your people what it is like to be truly loved.

Ha-Melitz will accompany you and he will take care of you as before. My son will come one night to receive you as his bride. I have prayed about this, and I believe your people need to see what redemption looks like."

Tamar's head was swimming now, *"I'm afraid. They will mock me and ridicule me and Jedidiah. I know them; they will not accept me back. They will never understand your forgiveness or his sacrifice my lord."*

She was pleading now. She knew her voice was strained but her fear was real. The people in Dannah had no more of an understanding about redemption than she had had. If she had not received it and lived it, she wouldn't have understood it either.

Abiel understood her struggle. It was more than the shame she would face by returning home; she would be trying to explain something totally foreign to her people.

Slowly he spoke, *"You know, this is like a foreign language to them. No one learns a new language in a day. It takes time. The time that you are waiting for my son to come and receive you should be spent teaching them what you have learned."*

Tamar swallowed hard; she would rather take another beating than to face her own people again.

"I don't think I can do this that you ask my lord. Please forgive me, but this is too hard for me to do" Tamar said as she unconsciously clenched her fist.

Abiel could see the turmoil going on inside of Tamar, and he knew the fear and pain that she was feeling was real.

Still, if she hid from her past, it would surely reappear some day when she was unprepared to face it. She would be better to face it head on, and be done with it forever.

"My child, you offered to die if I asked you to. You promised that you would do anything I asked you to do. Didn't you? You said that your life belonged to my son, and was not your own, remember? Abiel gently reminded her of what she had promised.

His words stung her deeply. She knew that her own words were now convicting her.

Tearfully she answered him, *"I am your servant. I will do anything you ask of me. Only I beg of you, don't forsake me now."*

Abiel realized for the first time that Tamar still was fearful of being rejected. Somehow the devil had made her worry that even after all that had transpired she would be unwanted by Jedidiah. *"You will never be left alone or forsaken my daughter. Fear not. Only trust and believe."*

Suddenly a thought occurred to Tamar; why did Abiel care about her town? What did it matter if they understood true love or not? It wouldn't make his life any better or worse.

"May I ask you something?" she said as she stared into his eyes intently.

Abiel had not taken his eyes off of her.

"What is it you wish to know?" he asked.

"Why do you desire to teach the people of Dannah about love?" she questioned him.

It was a fair question to ask. Dannah was insignificant even to itself. No one there thought that they mattered in the grand scheme of things. What did it really matter what they believed?

"I guess to the world at large, Dannah and its people don't account for much do they?" he asked.

"No, not really they don't" she said.

"Do you think that God is aware of who lives in Dannah?" Abiel asked Tamar. *"Because I am sure that the God I serve not only is aware, but that He loves each and every one of them. From the best to the worst, God loves them all"* he answered confidently.

Abiel began to explain to Tamar a great truth about love.

"There are good and bad people in every village around the world. When people become convinced that evil is normal, they allow it to grow. The good becomes forgotten. We need for the people of Dannah to believe in the goodness of God. If their faith in God's faithfulness is revived it will change their lives. I have thought about my son's sacrifice for you. He saved you and for that I am thankful, but is that all that is to be gained from his sacrifice?

I believe that others need to see what he has done. Some will be encouraged, and they will start to believe in the power of love. Maybe a few lives will be affected this way. Some will never believe. We cannot make them change. But Tamar, love has the potential to change the world if we let it. Those of us who have experience true love know that it is stronger than death and stronger than hate. Tamar, you must understand this; God is love, and until we learn to show love like He shows love we will never be like Him. I am asking you to be like God. Will you try to do this for me?"

"I will do everything that you ask me to do, even if it causes me to be despised, ridiculed and mocked" answered Tamar.

"It might. But I believe if even one soul is saved it is worth it" Abiel said.

Tamar had bowed her head to hide her face from Abiel. She didn't want him to see her tears or to see her look of fear. Gently lifting her chin with one hand, Abiel looked into her eyes again and smiled as he said, *"Now then, Ha-Melitz will accompany you home. And do not forget for even one moment that my son loves you, and I love you. One night soon he will return for you to rescue you from Dannah. He will come! Don't forget! Be watchful and ready!"*

Smiling weakly, Tamar promised that she would be ready.

Dannah was going through the motions of an ordinary day when Ha-Melitz and Tamar rode in. Every conversation immediately stopped as all eyes focused on the pair.

Tamar could feel her face flush with shame. In her mind she wished that she could have sneaked into town the way that she had once sneaked out.

Ha-Melitz could sense her uneasiness, *"It will be fine, trust me. You just focus on seeing your parents again. They have missed you. It will be fine, relax and trust me."*

His words were strong and they gave her strength. She knew that no matter how bad she had behaved, Ha-Melitz would fight to defend her.

Arriving at her parents' home, Tamar hesitated before dismounting her horse. Her father was a mean man on a good day. How would he act now after she had caused him such shame?

Hearing someone stop outside of their house, her mother Tirzah opened the door. Loammi had supposed it was one of his collectors so he sent her to see who it was. Tirzah could scarcely believe her eyes when she saw Tamar,

"Oh my daughter you are alive!" she said. *"Come inside. Your father will want to see you."*

Tamar took a deep breath and got down from the horse. Her mother threw her arms around her and led her inside of the house.

Loammi was sitting looking away from Tamar when she entered the room. She realized that he was going to shame her as much as possible. This would be her first battle, winning her own family.

Her father was the type of man who took delight in belittling others. This was going to be a difficult time for Tamar. But then she remembered Abiel's words and she thought, *"Maybe my own parents can change!"*

"Look who is here, it is Tamar our daughter!" said Tirzah. Loammi refused to acknowledge Tamar or to even look her way.

Tamar slowly made her way to her father. He was a horrible excuse for a father and she knew it. The only man who had ever been a father to her was Abiel. She would do what he told her to do, because as his daughter, it was her duty no matter the cost.

Bowing down beside him she said, *"Father, I have sinned before heaven and in your sight. I am no longer worthy to be called your child but I ask you to treat me as your servant please."*

"If you were my servant I would sell you to Othniel" he grumbled, *"If he would even have you."*

Looking her in the face he seemed to not notice the still present bruises on her cheeks or the signs of her lips being busted. He had wild eyes like an animal this day. It was obvious that he was already drinking.

"What you can do for me is to go away! Why have you returned? Haven't you caused your mother and I enough pain already? Where is your precious Ahaz now? " he yelled at the top of his voice.

"Father, haven't you heard?" she asked him.

Tirzah took Tamar's hand and asked, *"Heard what?"*

"I was tricked into going with Ahaz mother. He stole my money, and sold me into slavery in Raphia. But I was rescued by Jedidiah" she answered.

Her mother didn't reply, but she didn't need to. Tamar could tell by the looks on her parents faces that they had not heard the story of her remarkable rescue.

The truth was no one in Dannah knew her story. They all had heard that she ran away with Ahaz, but they knew nothing of her captivity in Raphia.

For Tamar the realization that she would have to explain her story made her feel even worse! She had expected that everyone already knew what had happened.

For a moment she considered telling only part of the story by making herself look innocent. It would be easy to make Ahaz the guilty party. Everyone would believe that, but it wasn't true. She knew that sooner or later the whole truth would come out.

It was like Abiel had said, *"It is better to face it head on and be done with it once and for all!"*

She would have to relive the whole ordeal of her betrayal of Jedidiah, and of her being betrayed by Ahaz.

She hated herself for what she had done. It caused her grief to even admit it to herself, but to go over it again and again to her friends would be torture. To know that they would be speaking of it in their homes was too much for her to bear.

For a brief moment she thought, *"Why would Abiel send me home so I could go through this if he really loves me like a daughter?"*

But one thing that she knew for certain was that Abiel and Jedidiah truly did love her. She knew that they wanted only what was best for her.

If they would take her back after she was defiled by Salah and his family, how could she not trust them now?

"Trust!" that was the one word that Tamar kept repeating in her mind. Trust that Abiel loved her like a daughter even if her father did not.

Trust that one day soon Jedidiah would come for her just as he promised that he would do.

Trust that Ha-Melitz would stay with her through all of her struggles. He sought her out and found her. She knew that he would not forsake her now.

And what about God? He had orchestrated everything to her good. Even after she had messed up her life, God led Ha-Melitz to where she was. *"Just trust!"*

Sitting down beside her father she took his hands in hers and began to tell him her story. He remained unmoved throughout the story until she came to the part where Jedidiah took her place.

For the first time he seemed to come out of his stupor, *"He did what? Why would he take your place?"* he asked.

Tamar smiled, *"For love's sake papa, he and his father have a love for me that transcends anything I have ever even heard of. There is no greater love than what I have been shown.*

That is why I have come home. I know that you and mama have never experienced such love. It is God's love that they showed me. Papa, I want you to know God. I want you to know that He loves you and you can love Him."

Tamar felt that the Spirit of God was with her. Now she felt confidence in God. She knew that if God was on her side, everything would work out alright.

With a quizzical look her father stared into her eyes for several minutes. It occurred to Tamar that he was looking at her as if he had never really seen her before.

With wide eyes he said, *"You are not the daughter who ran away are you? God has changed you. Abiel and Jedidiah have changed you. My daughter acted selfish, like me. You have become someone else."*

Tamar began to weep, and to her astonishment so did her father and mother. They embraced for a long time; weeping at first, but then amazingly, they began to laugh.

Tirzah was the first to laugh. This was something that Tamar could not remember her mother ever doing. Then Tamar began to laugh, and then her father started laughing. He laughed so loud that he shook, and the laughing became contagious!

They all were laughing and none of them knew why the others were laughing.

Finally Loammi said through his laughter, *"I feel something in my soul that I have not felt since I was a young boy! The joy of the Lord is in my heart! I feel God! Oh Hallelujah!"*

Then it was that Tamar realized something; although her family talked about God and had always prayed to Him, none of them actually knew God.

They may as well have been speaking to the moon or a star when they prayed. They didn't actually know God. Her whole village was like that! That was why Abiel sent her home. She must tell them about God!

For the next few hours, Tamar related the entirety of her story. She had expected that she would feel depressed as she went over her failures and her imprisonment, but she didn't. Instead of focusing on how she had suffered, she focused on how her Redeemer had come.

She told the story of how he had stepped in to take her place and to bear her sin on his body.

Loammi and Tirzah sat and listened to her as she explained what Abiel told her. She told them of this great love that he said was the love of God for all people.

Then Loammi did something that Tamar did not expect to ever see in her lifetime; he bowed his head and asked God's forgiveness for his sins.

Tirzah was weeping with joy as she also prayed for forgiveness.

Loammi prayed this way, *"God our Father, I have sinned against you for many years. I am so unworthy of your mercy. When I was a small boy I lost my mother and I blamed you. I have been bitter against you all of these years. I realize now that it was your mercy that kept me alive so that I could repent and come to know you. Thank you Father God!"*

Tamar had never pitied Loammi. To her he was just a mean drunk who happened to be her father. But now she looked at him with an overwhelming sense of pity.

She now saw him as a little boy who had lost his mother and was hurting inside. She remembered that his father had remarried to a cruel woman that hated Loammi. He had suffered much at her hands when he was young. This was the first time since he was a child that he had admitted his hurt.

All of those years of holding it inside had made him bitter. Now it was as if a flood-gate had been opened and he couldn't stop it; he didn't want to stop it either! The joy of the Lord was his strength.

Smiling broadly he took Tamar's hands in his and said, *"When I was little I loved the Lord, Tamar. But when my mother passed away and my father shoved me aside, I blamed God. But He loved me enough to let me live long enough so that He could reach me with the good news. How could I ever deny Him?"*

Tamar realized that this was the first time in her entire life that her family was happy! How strange it seemed that they were laughing and rejoicing in what had always been a sad house! *"Oh papa, I love you and mama. I am so glad that I was able to come home."*

Tirzah had not said much. In many ways she had suffered the most. When Tamar had ran away it wasn't Loammi who had to shop for food and hear the remarks, it was Tirzah. She was the one who had to bear the constant ridicule and mocking.

For years she had been forced to deal with a husband who was a mean drunk. Then her only child had shamed her. She had never liked Dannah. It was his town, not hers. She had come from northern Israel. The people were different there. For many years she had been alone here with just a shy daughter to keep her company.

Then when Tamar had run away, Tirzah wished that she could have left Dannah too. All of the suffering in silence had taken its toll on her. But she too was feeling the Lord's Spirit in her heart.

For the first time since she was young, she felt peace in her home. Whatever this was, she never wanted it to leave.

Speaking to Tamar she said, *"I have never known God before. My family never worshipped him and I only prayed to Him when I really was worried about something. Today I have asked His forgiveness and a strange, wonderful feeling swept over me! Is this love?"*

"Yes mama, it is love. The whole world may turn against a child of God, but God will never leave us or forsake us" answered Tamar.

It suddenly occurred to Tamar that she was leading her family to God and she barely knew Him herself. There was far more that she didn't know than what she did know.

Just then a thought occurred to Tamar, *"You know how Ha-Melitz has always been here because he is the best friend of Jedidiah? God has promised that His Spirit will always be with us to help us. His Spirit acts as the best man. He brings us to the Father."*

The rest of the evening was spent rejoicing and, Tamar realized, getting to know each other.

Although she had been raised in this home, there was so much that she did not know about her parents. And there was much that they didn't know about each other.

It was two days before Tamar summoned the courage to go to the market place. Tirzah walked with her to give her strength. About half-way to the market Tamar turned to go back home. That was when Ha-Melitz called her name. Turning, she saw him smiling; he was going to accompany her to the market. Once again feeling confident, she began to walk towards the crowd of people who were watching her.

She was nervous and wondering how to start a conversation with one of the vendors when someone spoke from behind her.

"Look what came crawling back to Dannah! I hear that you are looking for a new husband!"

Turning to see who spoke those words she was startled to see Othniel standing there.

His voice sounded different to Tamar. It was deeper and sounded even more wicked than she remembered it.

"No, I am married to Jedidiah, son of Abiel, Othniel. I am awaiting my husband's return. He will come soon and take me to Jerusalem" she spoke firmly to him.

When she first started to speak a feeling of fear had gripped her, but when she mentioned Jedidiah's name she felt courage and strength come into her voice. No matter what anyone in Dannah thought, she knew that he loved her.

Othniel mocked her, *"Who is going to believe that story now? We all have heard that you ran away with Ahaz. What's the matter? Did he change his mind?"*

The crowd was gathering and Tamar realized that now was as good of a time as any to tell her story. Tirzah took her hand and squeezed it gently as if to say, *"I am with you."*

Then she began to tell her story. Othniel and some of the others would interrupt her occasionally, but she kept speaking.

Then when she got to part where she was betrayed by Ahaz, Othniel began to mock her.

"I don't believe you! I bet you left Ahaz. You probably enjoyed the boy in Raphia didn't you?" he said.

His words stung Tamar, but she kept telling what happened in spite of his interruptions. Ha-Melitz was standing close enough so that Tamar could see his face at all times. His presence gave her the confidence she needed.

When she came to the part of her story where she was arrested and convicted for stabbing Salah the crowd became very silent. Not even Othniel knew what to say.

"I was about to be beaten to death and I knew it. I was so afraid to die, but I wanted to die to escape my private hell. Then I heard the voice of my beloved speak. He interrupted my punishment and took my place. He bore my sins and my failures on his body.

These past few weeks I have spent in the healing house in Succoth with Abiel the father of Jedidiah.

After I was healed and Jedidiah was almost well, Abiel asked me to come back to Dannah. He desired that I tell you how God sent me a redeemer. And he asked me to tell you that this same God loves each and every one of you too!

You can know Him today if you will just repent of your sins and ask His forgiveness.

My father and mother have experienced His love, and God has healed my family. And I would love for all of you to know God today. How many of you want to know God and experience His love for yourself?"

Tamar stopped and surveyed the crowd. She realized that although she had known most of them her whole life, she didn't really know them at all.

As she looked each one in the eyes she noticed that some eyes had tears in them. She could sense that they felt hope. For many, this was the first time that anyone had told them that God loved them. Tamar guessed that over half of those in the market that day were genuinely touched by God.

Many in Dannah asked God to come into their lives that day. It was the beginning of a great change that altered the destinies of many people.

For the next few months Tamar and her family were busy being evangelists to the town of Dannah. Ha-Melitz was able to give them sound advice, for he was so close to Abiel and Jedidiah that he knew more about God than anyone else in Dannah.

Ahaz's family refused to change. And so did Othniel and his family, but most did change. Dannah took on a new spirit after that. It seemed that everyone was happier and friendlier than they had ever been.

Tamar was very happy with what God had done in her family and home town.

And of course Tamar was getting ready to be married soon. This time she did not complain about the wait.

If it took another year she would never complain again.

Tamar knew from Ha-Melitz that Jedidiah had to relearn to walk again after the whipping post. His recovery was progressing slowly but surely.

"I have spoken to Jedidiah on several occasions and I assure you that he is anxious to see you. His love for you has not diminished in the least. In fact, I think it is stronger today than it has ever been" Ha-Melitz told her.

"Soon" she told herself, *"Soon!"*

Chapter ten: The wedding

During her first engagement to Jedidiah, Tamar didn't have enough friends for a proper bridal party. But now, after all that God had done in Dannah she had too many! There were so many young girls who wanted to be her friend that Tamar ended up inviting all of them.

Ha-Melitz had given her hints that the day was at hand. She realized that at any moment Jedidiah would appear with his wedding party to take her to his father's house.

The last message that Ha-Melitz had given her from Jedidiah was for her to be ready and alert. All things were now ready. All that he needed was for his father to say, *"Go! Get your bride!"*

Before she lay down for the night she said a prayer, asking God to let it be tonight.

God had heard her prayer of course, He always hears our prayers.

In Jerusalem Abiel had been busy that day inspecting Jedidiah's Chador and the Huppah. He was satisfied that all things were now ready for the wedding. His son was whole and the meal was prepared. This would be a feast to be remembered for many years!

Jedidiah was watching his father make his rounds, *"Well father, what are you thinking?"* he asked.

Abiel stood still for several minutes, and then he spoke, *"I think it is time to bring your bride home!"* he answered. *"All things are prepared. I will send my servants with you; gather your friends and rescue your bride tonight!"*

Jedidiah leaped for joy at his father's news. Hugging Abiel he turned towards the house and ran to change into his wedding garment. All of his friends would also need to be alerted of the news. They too would have to change into their wedding garments. They would also have to get their horses ready for the long ride ahead of them.

It was over an hour later when they were finally ready to go. It was a very happy group who were assembled in front of Abiel's house that night.

Mounting his white stallion Jedidiah led his wedding party out of the gates of Jerusalem south towards Dannah. His story of love and redemption had been told and retold in the city.

Many of those who accompanied him went out of curiosity to see this girl who was worth the price that he had paid for her.

Bearing torches to light their way they rode the south road towards Bethlehem. Then they would take the southwest road to Dannah. It would take several hours to arrive in Dannah. Then they would have to have the stamina for the return trip.

As they drew near to Dannah, Jedidiah could feel his heart starting to beat faster with anticipation. The last time that he had seen Tamar, her face was still badly bruised. In his mind he imagined what she would look like now.

He remembered the first time that they had seen each other face to face, and how he felt at that moment. He especially remembered when they had held hands the first time. It reminded him of the Bible story of Ruth.

Ruth had been an outcast. She was from Moab, and they were cursed by God because of the way that they treated Israel in the Wilderness.

It was in Moab that she married a man from Judah. Her husband had died and so had his father and brother. Her mother in law Naomi was determined to return to Judah and die among her own people. Ruth loved her so much that she went with her back to Judah to the town of Bethlehem.

It was in Bethlehem that she met an honorable man named Boaz. One night Ruth slipped into the threshing floor where Boaz was sleeping and pulled back his robe, uncovering his feet.

Boaz awoke and realized it was her. He could have taken advantage of her, but he was too honorable of a man to do that. He sent her home with enough grain to feed herself and her mother in law.

But Boaz couldn't sleep any more that night! That first touch had changed him forever. He was a near-kinsman to Ruth's departed husband, so he had a legal claim to have her as his wife. But there was another man who also had a claim, and he was even nearer kin than Boaz.

Before the sun set the next day he had bought the right to marry Ruth from the man who was nearer kin.

It was the first touch that caused Boaz to do everything to win Ruth. It was the same with Jedidiah; he never got over that feeling of the first time he held hands with Tamar.

When they were within sight of Dannah he had instructed his friends to blow the trumpets and to make the proclamation, *"Behold, the bridegroom comes, go you out to meet him!"*

As they neared the edge of the town Jedidiah caused the procession to pause. He wanted to savor this moment. These months had been difficult for him too. He had been ready weeks ago, but he had to wait until his father said it was time.

Finally Jedidiah was ready, *"Blow the trumpets and shout!"* he yelled, *"Awaken my bride!"*

For the entire distance from Jerusalem to Dannah the group had been in a celebratory mood, but now they really got excited!

The trumpeters summoned all of their strength, and every bit of breath, to make the trumpets as loud as humanly possible.

In Dannah nearly everyone had been asleep for a few hours. When the trumpets sounded the whole town awoke at the same instance.

Even though all of them knew that this time was coming some of them were not prepared for it. They knew that this was a once in a lifetime event. They would never get another chance to participate in such a spectacle. Yet several of them had let their lamps burn out, and some did not have their wedding garments ready.

As soon as they heard the trumpets sounding they began to run around trying to get ready, but it was already too late. By the time that they had lit their lamps, gathered their belongings and filled their vessels with oil Jedidiah and Tamar would have left.

Jedidiah was hurriedly riding his horse into town. Alongside of him was another horse for Tamar.

When the groom's party arrived at the bride's house there was a symbolic ransoming of the bride. This was an old tradition in Israel that brought back memories of God ransoming Israel from Egyptian bondage.

As Israel had been delivered from being slaves, the new bride was delivered from being bound to her old life.

From this day forward she and her husband would be one in God's sight. Her only bondage was the love bond between husband and wife.

Tamar and her parents awoke with a start at the sounding of the first trumpet. *"Praise God! That was a trumpet!"* she shouted.

Loammi opened the door to look towards the sound and saw the torchlight procession moving his way. *"Tamar he comes! Get your things! Your husband approaches!"* he said.

By this time Tamar had combed her hair and put on her gown. Quickly she bound up her few belongings that Jedidiah had given to her and stood waiting. In just a few minutes he would knock on her door and call her name.

When he did she would open the door to him and take his hand. Nervously she looked down at her hand and realized that it was sweaty! *"Oh Lord have mercy on me! I am so nervous I don't know what to do!"* she said.

Every house in town was now lit up. Each doorway had at least one head peering out. They had known that Tamar's husband was coming someday, but sadly some of them didn't believe it would be this night.

This was literally a once in a lifetime occurrence in their small village. Those who had prepared would be allowed to go to the capital city! The king and his family would be there. It was a great honor to be invited, and all they had to do was to be ready!

The young ladies who were accompanying Tamar to the wedding were grabbing their lamps. It was a long way to Jerusalem and they would have to keep up. Tamar's father and mother also were getting ready.

Jedidiah only came for one person and that was Tamar! Anybody else who came would have to be ready when the bride and groom left, and they would have to keep up. The wedding party was not going to stop along the way and rest! This was a one-way trip to Jerusalem.

Tamar held her breath as she heard the sound of the horses approaching her house. Over the shouting and the trumpets she could hear Jedidiah dismount. Step by step he came and then he firmly knocked on her door!

"Are you home my beloved?" he called. *"And are you ready to come with me?"*

"I am home my love, and I am most anxious to go with you" she replied.

Opening the door he looked into her face. The first thing he noticed was her eyes. They sparkled in the torchlight and he couldn't help but think of how much he loved looking into her eyes.

Then he reached out and took her by her hand, *"Come, my father's house is ready. My Huppah is finished. My Chador is also ready. All things are prepared for you."*

Standing next to him was his faithful friend Ha-Melitz smiling. His work was now finished. He was relieved to be free from the work of getting the bride ready. Now he could rejoice in the fact that his friend was happy.

Jedidiah had also brought two horses for Tamar's parents to ride. This was a great honor for them, and especially her mother who had never ridden a horse.

He helped Tamar to get on her horse as his friends helped her parents to mount theirs. Then surveying the crowd he cried out, *"Come with me my friends to the Marriage Supper!"*

It was a long and noisy ride back to Jerusalem as the crowd shouted and sang for joy. The happy couple rode side by side holding hands as they did.

In Jerusalem Abiel was making sure everything was ready. He checked each item carefully because they all held special significance to the Jews.

As they reached Abiel's house, Tamar and Jedidiah joyfully dismounted their horses as the people gathered around them. There were literally thousands of guests who had come.

As they walked, hand in hand, they were first greeted by Abiel. He was smiling brightly as he welcomed them home.

Sitting in the chairs the crowd cheered wildly; they were now the king and queen of the wedding!

Jedidiah's closest friends picked them up in their chairs and carried them into the home. As they were lifted up, they held hands all the way to the Huppah.

When the chairs were at the correct place they were carefully lowered and then Jedidiah and Tamar stood together before the priest.

Before the Huppah ceremony, the groom, escorted by his father and (about to become) father-in-law, and accompanied by relatives and friends, went forward to veil the bride.

The groom brought down the veil over the bride's face, reminiscent of Rebekah's covering her face with her veil upon seeing Isaac before their marriage.

The veiling impresses upon the bride her duty to live up to Jewish ideals of modesty. It also reminds others that in her status as a married woman she will be absolutely unapproachable by other men.

For Tamar, it was not necessary for her to be reminded that she was married. Her husband was the greatest man on earth as far as she was concerned. She would never again look at another.

The groom and the bride were both dressed in dazzling white robes. The Huppah was set up in the courtyard behind Abiel's house.

Before they go to the Huppah all the knots on the groom's garments are untied. This symbolizes that at the moment of marriage all other bonds are broken. The only bond that he is beholding to is the one between him and his bride.

Upon arriving at the groom's home the guests would have two chairs waiting side by side. One was for Jedidiah and the other one was for Tamar. They would be seated and the guests would pick them up and carry them to the Huppah.

There was a curtain hung to keep them separated, but they were able to hold hands when they were lifted up.

This was the first time that Tamar had seen the Huppah, and she was awestruck. Jedidiah had made it to honor her and he had done marvelously!

It had her favorite colors in it and was made of the priciest cloth available. It was the most beautiful thing she had ever seen.

Turning towards Jedidiah and looking in his eyes she started crying. “I love you!” seemed to be not enough. She wanted so badly to be able to make him feel what was in her heart at that moment. Words just couldn’t convey her emotions.

The priest then pronounced the seven blessings upon them.

“Praised are You, O Lord our God, King of the Universe, Creator of the fruit of the vine. Praised are You, O Lord our God, King of the Universe, Who created all things for Your glory. Praised are You, O Lord our God, King of the Universe, Creator of man. Praised are You, O Lord our God, King of the Universe, Who created man and woman in Your image, fashioning woman from man as his mate, that together they might perpetuate life. Praised are You, O Lord, Creator of man. May Zion rejoice as her children are restored to her in joy. Praised are You, O Lord, Who causes Zion to rejoice at her children’s return.”

“Grant perfect joy to these loving companions, as You did to the first man and woman in the Garden of Eden. Praised are You, O Lord, who grants the joy of bride and groom.” “Praised are You, O Lord our God, King of the Universe, who created joy and gladness, bride and groom, mirth, song, delight and rejoicing, love and harmony, peace and companionship.

O Lord our God, may there ever be heard in the cities of Judah and in the streets of Jerusalem voices of joy and gladness, voices of bride and groom, the jubilant voices of those joined in marriage under the bridal canopy, the voices of young people feasting and singing. Praised are You, O Lord, Who causes the groom to rejoice with his bride."

The blessings of the Jews had more to do with God than it did with the couple. That was because they recognized that without God there could be no marriage. And they knew that without His protection a marriage would not last.

As he recited these blessings the priest held up a cup of new wine to God. When he was finished he handed the cup to the bride and the groom.

Each took a drink from the cup. **This was the second cup.** They drank the first cup together at the time of their engagement meal. The Kiddushin cup signified that the previous promises that were made were still in effect. The covenant was still valid.

After they drank the Kiddushin cup, Jedidiah handed it back to the priest.

The wedding ceremony took place under the open sky. This is in remembrance of God's promise to Abraham that his descendants would be as numerous as the stars of heaven. God said this to Abraham when it appeared he would die childless.

This reinforces to the couple that not only is God watching over the ceremony, but He is their real source in life. And that it is from God that all blessings come. The Psalmist said that even children were part of the heritage of the Lord.

The Huppah reminds the bride of how Ruth said to Boaz, *"spread your robe over your handmaid."* As she was willing to submit to her lord Boaz, Tamar was to submit to Jedidiah.

Escorted by his father and father-in-law, Jedidiah was the first to step into the Huppah. He is first to signify that he is providing the covering for his wife.

Escorted by her mother and other women Tamar then stepped in. Taking her by the hand Jedidiah then turned facing the priest. This signifies Tamar's transition from her parents' home to Jedidiah's.

Jedidiah quoted a portion of the Royal Wedding Psalm to Tamar;

"My lady, listen to me. Listen carefully and understand me. Forget your people and your father's family, so that the king will be pleased with your beauty. He will be your new husband, so you must honor him. People from Tyre will bring you gifts. Their richest people will try to win your friendship. The princess is so beautiful in her gown, like a pearl set in gold. Clothed in beauty, she is led to the king, followed by her bridesmaids." **Psalms 45:10-14**

Jedidiah and Tamar were the king and queen this day, and forever would she consider him her king and lord.

The wedding vows were then spoken. Jedidiah went first, and then Tamar spoke her vows.

The priest again proclaimed the seven blessings.

When he finished the whole company erupted into cheers as the trumpets again blew loudly. It seemed to Tamar that everyone in Jerusalem must be at their wedding.

Jedidiah led Tamar by the hand to the head table. There they sat as the king and queen of the marriage feast.

Ha-Melitz and Abiel were both overcome with joy. This day had seemed to be an impossibility at one time, but now it was a reality.

The priest then came forward to proclaim a blessing over the meal. As they bowed their heads for the blessing, Tamar quietly thanked God for all that He had done for her.

Then after saying grace over the meal, the priest held up a cup of new wine. Handing this cup to Jedidiah, he and Tamar drank from it. **This was the third cup that they drink together.**

Each of the cups represented something to the Jews. The fourth was saved to be shared in private between the husband and his bride in the Chador.

The first cup was the cup of sanctification. Sanctification means to be chosen, cleansed and set-apart. When Tamar and Jedidiah shared the first cup on the night they met she agreed to be only his.

The second cup that they shared was called the cup of deliverance. They drank this cup when they returned to Jerusalem the night that he went to Dannah with the wedding party. Tamar was delivered from her former life just as the Israelites had been delivered from Egyptian bondage.

The third cup was the cup of redemption; they drank this cup when they were seated together as king and queen of the marriage supper.

The fourth cup is called the cup of hope. They drink this alone in the honeymoon chamber called the Chador.

Jedidiah entered the chamber first. This represents that he is the owner of the home and its protector. Then the bride enters. This proclaims publicly that he is responsible for her protection.

They then partake of the fourth cup. This cup is the seal of their marriage.

Tamar and Jedidiah seemed to float through much of the ceremony. It all went so fast for Tamar that she hardly had time to think. All that she could do was react when it was time to and recite what she was told to recite.

Amidst the cheering of the crowd and the families the happy couple went to the honeymoon chamber and closed the door. From this point on they were no longer two people but one.

All of this pageantry was necessary and important. To a Jew it would have served as a history lesson reminding everybody of what God has done for his people. God made specific promises to the people of Israel and His good Word was performed to the letter.

To the Jew God was more than just the Almighty, He was also the Faithful and True God, full of compassion and mercy. The foundation of the marriage was not based on the love of man and woman, but the love of God for mankind.

Epilogue A family is born

Many years passed, and Tamar and Jedidiah remained in love throughout. Children were born to them, and Tamar was happy being Jedidiah's wife.

As the years passed by, Jedidiah's looks began to fade. His scars became more noticeable and his face became even more disfigured. Every once in a while some man would try to steal Tamar from Jedidiah. He would start by telling her that she could have done better, or that she was too pretty for such an ugly man.

This always caused Tamar to laugh in the person's face that said it. She would tell them what she told everyone;

"Do you see those scars? To you they may look ugly, but to me they are beautiful. I should have been the one to wear those scars. It should have been me that was beaten so badly. It should have been my blood that was spilled that day. My husband took my place and bore my punishment. He is perfect just as he is, and you cannot come close to being as perfect as Jedidiah son of Abiel."

Those who knew her best also knew that there was no way she would ever hurt Jedidiah again. But she loved to tell the story of her husband's love for her. She came to love the scars he bore.

As the children grew they too became aware of the story of their father's sacrifice. Rather than being ashamed of his looks, they were proud to tell what happened. Their father gladly bore their mother's suffering!

Tamar lived with the knowledge that she was loved. That doesn't mean that she never had fears or nightmares. The past did continue to haunt her from time to time.

Her nightmares were of two sorts;

She would dream that she was being held captive again. She usually woke up screaming from that type of dream.

Or she would have a nightmare in which Jedidiah was angry with her, and that he blamed her for his pain and suffering. If she allowed it to, this dream would make her depressed and fearful.

But Jedidiah recognized the suffering in his wife's soul. He would give her constant reaffirmation that he loved her.

The problem with sin is that it scars whatever it touches. It scarred Tamar inside. It scarred Jedidiah on the outside. Sin destroys everything it touches.

The story however does end well. The sufferings of the bride and the groom became legendary. The fact that a man would sacrifice so much for the one that he loved inspired others to believe.

Many people came to recognize that there was something greater and stronger than death, and it was love.

This great truth revolutionized many lives and it still is a revolutionary truth to this day; there is a love that is stronger than any force on earth.

That wonderful kind of love was shown when God the Father sent His precious Son to die for mankind. He took our punishment so that we could go free. Now we owe Him a tremendous love-debt.

From the Pastor: God's plan

Tamar's story is really our story. All of us have stories of pain and suffering. We all know what it is like to battle loneliness and depression. Sooner or later almost everyone faces the demon of hopelessness.

But God loves us! He is always searching for that lost one that He can bring into His family.

He chose us to be the bride of Christ! This is our ***Shiddukhin.***

He made us a great offer of salvation if we will only accept it. This is our ***Ketubbah***.

He sent His Holy Spirit, the Comforter, to help us. He is our ***Ha-Melitz***, our Helper.

He gave us our ***Mohar***, the bride price, when He gave us His only Son to pay our sin debt on the cross. Now there is no more debt to be paid except the love debt we owe to Christ our Groom.

The Son provided us the ***Mattan***, the love gifts, by sending us the Gifts of the Spirit to perfect us, and to get us ready to meet our heavenly Bridegroom. As long as the church remains on this earth it will need these gifts, and they will be available to her.

We are now in the period of time where we prove our love and devotion to the Groom. It is our ***Kiddushin***. The believer must be faithful to Jesus.

Just as Tamar failed Jedidiah, many of us fail Christ.

However Christ knows our frame, He knows that we are but dust! If we will repent, which means to be sorrowful and to turn away from our sins, He will forgive us.

He wants to have fellowship with His bride. It is up to us to keep that relationship alive. Jesus cannot do any more than what He has already done.

Soon the Father will say that it is time, and the Groom will come for His bride. That will be our ***Nissuin.*** This includes what we call the rapture of the church, the Wedding of the Bride and Groom, the Marriage Supper, and also the Judgement Seat of Christ. The Nissuin transpires in heaven.

The meanings of the names:

Abiel means "God is my father"

Jedidiah means "Beloved of the Lord"

Ha-Melitz means "The Comforter"

Dannah means "He (God) will judge"

Loammi means "Not my people"

Tirzah means "She is my delight"

Tamar means "date-palm" a type of palm tree whose branches were used to lay before Christ during His triumphant entry on Palm Sunday

Amnon means "Faithful"

Salah means "To attack, to spear"

Succoth means "Booth or shelter"

You may correspond with Pastor Derek Jones via e-mail at revdcj@yahoo.com or by writing him at PO box 253 Desoto Mo. 63020

Cover design by Pastor Derek Jones

Model; Taylor Jones

76945632R00093

Made in the USA
Columbia, SC
27 September 2019